ABOVE ALL ELSE

JEFF ROSS

ORCA BOOK PUBLISHERS

Library and Archives Canada Cataloguing in Publication

Ross, Jeff, 1973-, author
Above all else / Jeff Ross.
(Orca sports)

Issued in print and electronic formats.
ISBN 978-1-4598-0388-6 (pbk.).--ISBN 978-1-4598-0389-3 (pdf).--
ISBN 978-1-4598-0390-9 (epub)

I. Title. II. Series: Orca sports
PS8635.O6928A76 2014   jC813'.6   C2013-906730-2
C2013-906731-0

First published in the United States, 2014
Library of Congress Control Number: 2013951371

Summary: Del tries to figure out who is responsible for injuring his teammate
when winning takes priority on the Cardinals soccer team.

MIX
Paper from
responsible sources
FSC
www.fsc.org   FSC® C016245

*Orca Book Publishers is dedicated to preserving the environment and has printed
this book on Forest Stewardship Council® certified paper.*

Orca Book Publishers gratefully acknowledges the support for its publishing
programs provided by the following agencies: the Government of Canada through
the Canada Book Fund and the Canada Council for the Arts, and the Province of
British Columbia through the BC Arts Council and
the Book Publishing Tax Credit.

Cover photography by Corbis Images
Author photo by Simon Bell

ORCA BOOK PUBLISHERS
PO Box 5626, Stn. B
Victoria, BC Canada
V8R 6S4

ORCA BOOK PUBLISHERS
PO Box 468
Custer, WA USA
98240-0468

www.orcabook.com
Printed and bound in Canada.

17 16 15 14 • 4 3 2 1

As always, for Megan.

chapter one

"We got this one, guys!" Jared Haynes said. Then he began slapping his shin pads in the quick way he did before every game. Next he would fiddle with his necklace before taking it off and looping it around itself three times. Finally, he would start pacing the room, his head bobbing from side to side.

"Number one, guys," Osmund (Oz) Clarke said on cue. It was as if they were reading from a script. Nothing changed game after game. Normally, I would have

1

tried to get changed and out onto the field as quickly as possible. But as the season wound down, Coach Dolan had demanded that everyone remain in the locker room until the last second. No exceptions. The idea was that we came out as a team, so we would play like a team.

The reality, however, was that I was forced to suffer through this garbage.

"Hey, Oz," Jared said, flicking a ball to him.

"Yeah, mon," Oz replied. Oz is half Jamaican, half white. If he were a coffee, he'd be heavily creamed. I'm on the other end of the color spectrum. My mother is Dutch, and my father's family is Swedish. It's as if the sun spotted us one day, then said, "All right, that's enough" and never returned.

"What's second place, Oz?"

"Second place, mon?"

"Yeah. *Second* place."

"Last time I checked, second place was the first loser."

"Damn straight, Oz." They slapped hands as a portion of the locker room settled into a chant of "losers, losers, Heighton ain't no losers."

"These guys are going down," Oz said, standing up and thumping his chest against Jared's.

"No doubt." The chanting moved to a steady, rhythmic "We're number one!" I wished I could just get out of the room. It was ridiculous to watch. Sure, Heighton High's soccer team hadn't lost a match in almost three years. This was the final game of the season. I wasn't on the team the first year, but I was the second, and I'll admit, winning feels great. It felt like we were a part of something bigger than all of us. Going undefeated in any sport is unheard of. Somehow we had the right collection of players and, of course, the right coach. None of this dulled the pain of how annoying the whole "winning attitude" had become. It was as if we didn't just expect to win, we deserved it.

Don't get me wrong—I'm not a huge believer in "the end result of any game is to have fun." But *all* the fun was being sucked out of the games. And then there were the practices. I'd never spent so much time running drills, watching videos and endlessly lining up penalty shots in my life.

But winning had become part of our culture, and losing was no longer an option.

Personally, I blamed our football team. They sucked hard. They'd been sucking hard for years. So when the soccer team started on its incredible roll, the whole student body got behind us.

"We got this one, Del," Riley McCoy said. Riley and I had made the team together. We were two of only three sophomores who had broken in that year. The rest of the team was made up of seniors, all still around from that first flawless season.

"It's not going to be easy," I said.

"Another perfect season," Oz yelled. "Three in a row. Unheard of."

Coach Dolan stepped into the locker room. Dolan, apparently, had played for some club in England before he found himself on the bad side of a tackle and permanently messed up his knee. He became a teacher and followed his wife here for work. That was three years ago. Exactly the same time that the team's winning streak began.

"How are we today, lads?" Coach said.

"Fired up, Coach," Oz said.

"Good on you. What do we have in the tank?"

"Filled up, Coach!" everyone yelled. Dolan demanded that we call him Coach. Never Mr. Dolan or Coach Dolan. Just Coach. It was like a secret handshake when you passed him in the hallway. "What are we going to give?"

"All we have and more!"

"That's right, lads. That's right. I know you will." He put a foot up on one of the benches and took us all in. "Lads, we have a chance to do something special here today. No team has gone three straight seasons without a loss. I believe we can be the first. There's no *can* or *cannot* here. Not only is

5

losing not an option, it's not even a possi-bility." Most of the players were nodding to this. Grinning. Getting "geared up," as Coach would say.

"*Losing* ain't a word we even know!" Jared yelled.

"That's right, Jared. That word isn't part of this team's vocabulary."

"Damn straight," Oz said. He and Jared high-fived one another.

"Lads, I don't need to tell you that if we win today, we get a bye to the second round of the playoffs. We won't have to play useless first-round stuff. But I want you to erase that thought from your minds. All you need to think about when you get out on that pitch today is winning. From the first second to the end of stoppage time, you are only thinking of winning. Nothing else matters. Now, let's get out there and finish this season right." He clapped his hands, and everyone jumped up.

"Get a goal and you're a hero today, Del," Riley said to me. "You'll go down in history."

"You too, Riley."

"I'm defense, Del. You're a striker. The glory is all yours."

"We'll see," I said as we ran through the door.

chapter two

It wasn't exactly an ear-shattering roar that greeted us on the field, but it was something. There were about two hundred kids in the bleachers. Most of them got to their feet when we ran onto the field. It wasn't like in those big games you see on TV where the team comes out of a tunnel or anything. We actually had to run across a regular suburban street to get to the pitch. But we did come up right between the two sets of bleachers.

The Roland Hills Rebels were already out on the pitch in their blue-and-gold outfits. The gold sparkled in the late-day sun.

"They look like a glee squad waiting to audition for a talent show," Jared said. He was jogging onto the pitch beside me, his chest high. I could tell he was sucking his stomach in.

"Pretty fancy outfits," I said.

"Car-di-nals, Car-di-nals," the crowd chanted.

"We are going to massacre them, mon," Oz said. Most of the year, Oz said *mon* maybe twice a week. But his family goes to Jamaica every spring break, and he comes back sounding like he's been possessed by the ghost of Bob Marley.

The ref blew his whistle twice as we neared.

"I should have dropped the ball already," he said. The ref was this bald guy who worked at the hardware store one town over. He was way too serious about soccer. "The game was supposed to start two minutes ago."

"Sorry," Jared said. He put his hand out, and the ref shook it.

"The Rebels have won the flip. Their ball." Jared accepted this. Coming out at the last minute was a ploy to get the other team angry. Coach believed that a team angry at some little thing like punctuality was more likely to make bad decisions due to frustration. I thought the whole idea was ridiculous, though the other players were staring us down and shaking their heads in annoyance.

The ref blew the whistle twice more as we scurried into position.

I play striker, so I didn't have far to go. The Rebels center kicked the ball back, and they quickly fell into a defensive structure. We had already played them once this season and managed to squeak out a win. It was very close though and ended up being their only loss of the season. That game could have gone either way.

So could this one.

The Rebels passed the ball around a lot. Back and forth. Round and round.

It seemed as if they were endlessly attempting to set up the perfect play. The problem with waiting for the perfect play is that you have to hope the other team falls out of position—which we rarely do.

Sometimes I rushed to intercept a pass or pressure one of the opposing strikers. Twice they kicked the ball back to their goalie, who then hoofed it upfield again. After about five minutes, it began to feel like one of those boring, inactive games that gives soccer a bad name.

"Come on," Jared called from the midfield. "Let's get this thing going." I was pretty sure the Rebels' technique was to lull us into a semi-comatose state and then try to sneak up to our net.

"Someone rush them," Romano said.

"Chill, Rom," Oz called.

The lead striker for the Rebels, Tim Irvine, took a pass off the right wing and started running the ball upfield. He passed Oz, who was too busy telling Rom to shut up, and easily deked Markus Miller, one of our midfielders.

Which left Rom.

Tim cut in toward the middle of the field before suddenly going back to the touch-line. He was almost past Rom when Rom performed a slide tackle, knocking the ball out of bounds and sending Tim flying.

"What the hell was that?" Tim said, getting up.

The ref was there immediately, a yellow card raised above him.

"I got the ball first," Rom said.

"You got my ankle first, asshole."

The ref blew the whistle again and waved the yellow card at Tim. Swearing during a game had been banned years before. Everyone knew it.

"Oh, come on," Tim said.

The ref grabbed the ball and waited for one player from each team to step up for a drop. Oz won the ball and quickly crossed it. Jared took the ball on the inside of his calf and started it upfield. The Rebels closed in quickly and somehow Jared managed to thread the needle and get a pass up to me. I tried to cross it back to Oz, but Tim got in the way, and the ball fell back into a muddle of kicking feet.

The game went that way for most of the first half. Back and forth. Running from one end to the other. The anticipation of a good setup or a possible corner kick—then nothing, the ball harmlessly booted down to the other end.

As time was running out on the first half, Oz and I managed to pass the Rebels midfielders in a quick give and go. Just inside the Rebels box, I swung out, then quickly cut back toward center. I faked a shot and crossed the ball back to Oz, who got up above his defender and headed it directly into the net.

I wouldn't say the crowd went wild, but the cheers were pretty loud. Oz came over and we high-fived. The whistle blew, and we left the field with a one-nothing lead.

On the sidelines, after giving Oz and me congratulatory claps on the back, Coach took Rom aside. I downed some water and a slice of orange. It seemed like Rom was getting an earful for his aggressiveness.

Though you never knew with Coach. It was entirely possible that he was praising Rom for his "intensity" and "need to win."

In the days after that game, with everything that happened, I thought back to that halftime and wondered what Coach had said to Rom. And if anything could have been different.

chapter three

"All right," Coach said, as the intermission came to a close. "Get back out there. And remember, you're playing to win, not to not lose."

The Rebels were going to have to play differently during this half. They needed a goal, so the sit-and-wait mentality wouldn't work.

They immediately began pressing. But that wasn't their style, and soon enough they were making wilder passes and coughing the ball up more frequently. Their coach started coming unglued on the sidelines. He kept yelling, "Control, control," until the ref came over and gave him a warning. The Rebels strikers began moving deeper into our end. Every time they did this, we pushed them back to half or let them play themselves into an offside. But with three of their players settled into our end, it left us with an opportunity to jump on any mistake they might make and have a nearly clear approach to their net.

Which was exactly what happened.

One of their midfielders tried to make a quick pass around Oz. But Oz is incredibly fast and managed to cut the pass off and tip it over to me. This time I had the whole left side clear. I ran the ball up the edge of the field. When a defender came in to intercept, I flicked the ball between his feet and kept moving. The defenders began shouting at one another. I could see Oz on the far side and Jared moving into the center. I had a head start on all of them, and only two defenders in my way. I got around one of the defenders as I neared the Rebels box and then, before the other defender could do anything, I bent over the ball and aimed squarely for the top left corner.

The ball arced up quickly and was on its way back down when it rang off the crossbar and shot straight back out onto the field. One of the Rebels defenders caught it with a quick header and sent it back to center, where a striker turned and blasted past our midfield. A quick give-and-go set him up for an easy tip-in.

Our keeper never had a chance.

I looked at our side, and we were in complete disarray. Everyone was out of position. This often happens when you get a good rush upfield. Everyone wants in on the action and moves farther forward, ready to keep the ball in play or quickly run up for a shot on net.

The Rebels celebrated as if they'd just won the World Cup.

"Look at those losers," Rom said. His face had gone a light pink. He was breathing heavily. "Man, I hate those guys."

"Bad bounce," I said. He turned his attention to me for a second. "It'll be the last one," he said, before trudging back to his defensive position.

What we had at the end of that game was a twenty-minute match. Neither team wanted the tie. It had nothing to do with the standings. Both teams just wanted to win.

Outside of our unbeaten record, a tie was as good as a win, because we had one more point than the Rebels. If the Rebels won, we would then each have a single loss. The problem was, we would end up in second place based on goal differential.

I checked Coach out as we lined up again. He was shaking his head. Beneath him was a stomped-on water bottle.

"Come on, guys!" Jared yelled, clapping his hands. "Get together!"

We moved quickly after the ref blew the whistle. Oz got the ball back to Jared, who then passed it on to another midfielder. This was a set play for us and likely the right decision at the time. We tried to move the other team side to side across the field until a lane opened.

In moments like this, I wished I could see the field from above. Like in a video game. When you're on the field, it's difficult to see which way everyone is moving. You might already have a lane and not know it. Or the other players could be closing in just as quickly.

Rom had the ball deep in our end. He spotted me upfield, deked out a rushing striker and hoofed the ball as hard as he could, trying to spring me. Rom is a decent defender. He can usually keep up with the opposing strikers and run them out of bounds or get in the way of a shot. But he has the worst long kick known to man. It's like he's trying to put the ball through a cloud or something. They always go almost straight up.

As this one did.

I started to run back to be part of the pack attempting to head the ball our way, but the wind caught the ball and shifted it across the field. It bounced behind Jared, and one of the Rebels strikers, a very talented kid named Doug Richards, brought it down on his chest and passed it right back to Tim.

Tim immediately pushed toward our box as Rom rushed him. Tim went head on into the challenge, probably thinking he could rotate around Rom at the last second. But even from where I was, I could see that Rom had no intention of going for the ball. In fact, he wasn't even looking at it. Rom charged and, as Tim began his rotation, jutted his leg out and caught him square on the knee.

Tim went down hard, both hands clasping his knee before he hit the ground. Rom hoofed the ball out of play just as Doug reached him.

Doug ran right into Rom and took him down. He managed to get four quick punches in before his own teammates pulled him off and the ref came in, blowing his whistle and waving red cards.

"The hell?" Rom said, holding his bloodied nose.

"That was intentional," Doug yelled. His teammates were holding him back. "Kick him out."

"You're both gone," the ref said, holding up two red cards. "One game each." Someone had brought the ball back to the field. The ref tucked it under his arm as Tim's teammates helped him off the field. He didn't seem to be able to walk on his own, and as he passed me, I could see his cheeks were streaked with tears.

"Penalty shot," the ref said. He dropped the ball, and everyone backed up. I thought Jared or Oz would complain about the penalty shot because Rom and Doug had both received red cards. It didn't make sense that there would be a penalty shot at all. But even they seemed stunned by what had happened.

The remaining Rebels striker, a kid named Michael, took the kick, and it was no contest. Penalty shots rarely are. The nets are just so huge. The ref blew the whistle and that was it. The Rebels had won.

We were going into the playoffs in second place for the first time in three seasons.

chapter four

After every big game, we go to Romano's
father's pizza parlor, Angelo's. It's not
exactly the most desirable restaurant
in town, but we eat for free, so no one
complains. The walls are covered in photos
of famous (Italian) soccer players. There are
newspaper articles and photos of our team
during the amazing two-year winning spree.

I was in a booth with Riley, Oz and
Romano. Jared came over with a chair turned
backward and sat down at the end of the table.

The smell of his cologne hovered in the air. He wore this really strong scent under the delusion that it drew women to him.

"So that was bullshit," Jared said.

"The hit?" Oz replied. Oz is a competitive player, but he believes in winning fairly.

"No, the penalty," Jared said.

Oz leaned back in his seat and pointed at Rom. "Rom says he was going for the ball."

"I was," Rom said.

"The *first* time you were going for the ball. But that next time, you were trying to hurt the guy," said Oz.

"I wasn't," Rom said. "Seriously, I got the ball first. I was just saying that if we had some kind of instant replay, everyone would see."

Jared looked at me. "You were right there. Did he get the ball first?"

"I didn't see," I lied.

"What were you looking at, Del?" Oz said.

"I guess the ball. But there was a defender in my way. I couldn't see everything that happened."

"Not that it matters," Jared interrupted. "What happened happened. Rom was being intense. He understands what *above all else* means, don't you, Rom?" Rom nodded, and Jared jammed a pizza crust into his mouth and talked around it. "That Irvine kid goes down too easy. He was hoping for the penalty shot."

"He's a good player," Riley said. "That's for sure."

"Yeah, yeah. Everyone's a good player. But he's a diver. He goes down four or five times a game. If he was a great player, he'd stay on his feet. Anyone heard if he's going to be back?" Jared said.

"I don't exactly chat with Roland Hills guys," Rom said.

"Yeah, who does?"

"He's out," Oz said.

"You call him or somethin'?" Jared said.

"No. But he went down hard. There's no way he's going to be back. He couldn't even walk off the field."

"Well, we'll see," Jared said. "It's still bullshit. That guy who punched Rom should have got a red card too."

"He did," I said.

"So where was our penalty shot?" Jared said.

"It happened in our end," I said. "I guess that's the way the ref saw it."

"The ref is blind. You know, he comes from over there."

"What do you mean?" Riley said.

"Roland Hills. He's not from here. That's his old school."

"He just called the play, Jared," Oz said. "I doubt he cares that much about which school wins."

"Why wouldn't he? That's his school."

Oz shrugged and finished his drink. "And Rom deserved everything he got. He played dirty and he got caught. So, what's done is done. Listen, I have to go." He slid out of the booth before anyone could reply. Most of the team had already left. It was a Friday night, and people had better things to do than sit around in a crappy pizza parlor.

"See you in the morning?" Jared said.

"What for?" Oz said.

"Coach called weekend practice. I just got the email."

"Man, I got stuff to do," Oz said.

"You want to be benched, then go ahead and don't show up."

Oz laughed. "He can't bench me. We've already got three guys injured. Now with Rom out, we only have one sub." He flexed his arms. "Besides, who could leave this kind of beauty off the field?"

"Ten AM, Oz," Jared said. Oz crossed the parlor and went outside, causing the little bell above the door to ring.

"I gotta go too," Riley said. He slapped me on the arm. "And Del's coming with me."

"I am?" I said.

"Yeah, remember?" He gave me a look that said "play along."

"Oh, yeah, for sure." I slid out of the booth.

"You'll both be at practice tomorrow morning?"

"For sure, Jare," I said. "Ten AM."

"Awesome." He put his fist out and I gave it a quick bump, an action that always made me feel like an idiot. I've tried to get into this whole sport-guy culture, and it just isn't me. I love soccer, but I leave it on the field. As for Jared, I always feel as if he's more into being an athlete than anything else. Like if the football or swim team were the ones doing well, he'd ditch soccer in a second and move on.

"Tomorrow," Riley said. He gave Jared an enthusiastic fist bump. Jared slid into the booth across from Rom and bent low over the table. As we were walking away, I heard Jared say, "Come on, man, tell me. What really happened out there?"

It was warm outside. The sun was going down, making everything around us glow. Riley had grabbed one of the soccer balls from the team bag and was bouncing it on the asphalt as we crossed the parking lot.

"Where are we going?" I asked.

"To meet a girl," Riley said.

"Oh yeah? So what do you need me along for?"

"She has a friend—you're my wingman."

"What girl?"

"Just this girl. I met her last week. I didn't get her number or anything, but she hangs out at the skate park."

"We're going to the skate park?"

"Yeah."

"So she's, what, a skater girl?"

"No. Maybe. I don't know."

"And her friend?"

"What about her?"

"What does she look like?"

"Not a clue, man. She just said she has a friend." Riley was a bit exasperating at times.

"We all have friends. Do you even know for sure that she'll be there?"

"No. But likely. She said she would." We were halfway to the park by this time.

"This is incredibly vague. You know that, right?" I said.

"She's cute," Riley said, then turned kind of pink.

"Well, that's good." I said. "Wait, which girl are you talking about?"

"Mine. Like I just said, I haven't seen yours."

"Now she's mine?" I said. "I think this relationship is moving too fast."

"Cute girls have cute friends. That's just how it works." He said it like it was the end of the conversation. "So, what do you really think about this whole Romano thing?"

"I think he did it on purpose. Actually, I know he did. I was five feet away when it happened."

"Why didn't you tell Jared when he asked, then?" Riley said.

"I didn't want to get into it," I said. Riley caught the ball on the side of his foot, and it shot into a hedge. He ran in, grabbed it and came back out to the sidewalk.

"And?" Riley said.

"And what?"

"Was it wrong?" I stopped walking. Riley took another couple of steps, then turned around. "What?"

"Are you serious?"

"Yeah. I mean, that Irvine guy is a dick. Like Jared said, he dives all over the place.

He'd already got one call to go his way. He's probably not even hurt."

"So you think Rom should have taken him out?"

"I think Rom was teaching him some respect."

I couldn't believe what Riley was saying. "Seriously?"

"I mean, I don't think it was totally the right thing to do. And, honestly, Rom is an idiot and easily the worst player on the team. But people have to learn some way, right?"

"Where is this coming from?" I said. Riley was normally a reasonable person.

"Jared and I used to be in martial arts together. At the place where we trained, anyone who did anything dishonorable was banned. It's not a bad policy."

"So, who in this situation is dishonorable? Rom or Tim?"

"Tim." I must have looked outraged, because Riley went on. "I'm not saying what Rom did was right. Okay? Just that it's one way to deal with people who try and play outside of the rules."

"Are you buying into this *above all else* stuff?"

"No. But I want to win. Don't you?"

"I want to play my ass off, yeah. And if we win, then good. But it's not what I play for."

"Really?" Riley said.

"No. How many people out there play as hard as they can and still lose?" Riley shook his head. "You have to play hard for yourself. That's all that matters. To always try and get better. Period."

"Sure, I guess. But I've done enough losing in my life." We'd started walking again. The heat was seeping out of the day. Cars flashed past.

"When do you ever lose? Soccer is all you play," I said.

"I used to skateboard—did you know that?"

"No."

"Well, that's because I sucked. And like I said, I used to do martial arts, but I sucked at that too. My grades are garbage this term. I don't have a job lined up for the summer or anything. My parents are going through a trial separation, and my sister is off at college getting, like, straight A's or whatever. This team is all I have at the moment. When we're winning, I feel like I'm doing something."

"Sure," I said. I'd had no idea all this was going on with Riley. We'd only begun hanging out the year before, when we both made the team. Before that, we'd moved in different circles.

"Anyway, you should care too. I hear scouts are going to show for the playoffs, and word is a few have their eye on you." I'd heard this as well. In fact, a couple of scouts had already contacted me. Soccer was becoming a real sport in North America, and there was money to be made. Talented players were starting to get serious scholarships.

"We'll see," I said. We were crossing the parking lot toward the skate park. "But let's agree that Romano is a dickhead."

"Oh, yeah. For sure. Who would debate that?"

I let a moment of silence pass between us. "Other than Romano?"

"Yeah, other than Romano."

"Maybe his dad."

Riley rubbed his chin. "Possibly. But highly unlikely."

chapter five

Our town's skate park is massive and seems to grow every year. It was built for this kid who was training a movie star for some film that, as far as I know, was never made. There had been a bunch of complaints about it too, since it sat right next to the beach and "ruined the atmosphere."

We walked around the whole mess once while Riley regaled me with tales of how he'd managed, or not, to land certain tricks in certain areas. We were behind the half-pipe when a girl came out of nowhere and punched him on the arm.

"You," she said.

"Oh, hey," Riley replied.

"Oh, hey yourself, we've been here for two hours. Where have you been?"

"I didn't know we had decided on a time to meet or..."

"We didn't? I totally thought we had." The girl was, as advertised, cute. She had wavy blond hair and clear blue eyes. Her clothes were fashionably torn. It seemed like she was wearing more makeup than a girl typically would for a night out at the skate park. But what did I know? Maybe that was how people always dressed here.

"This is Kira," Riley said. "Kira, Del."

"Oh yeah, for Elsa."

"For?" I said. Riley opened his mouth to speak, then just stood there silently. It was obvious that he was out of his depth with this girl. She was spontaneous, outgoing, the center of attention. Riley was more comfortable in the shadows.

"Well, not *for*. It's not like she's some kind of *gift*. I mean, get your mind out of the gutter. She's a fourth so you're not a third."

"A third?" I said.

"A third wheel." I looked at Riley again. I suddenly felt totally out of *my* depth. "Just wait a second," Kira said, and then she took off.

"What just happened?" I said.

"She's kind of all over the place."

"You think?"

Kira came out of a crowd of kids, whispering to a girl with dark-brown hair.

"Guys, this is Elsa," Kira said. "Elsa, this is Riley and *this* is Del."

"Hi," Elsa said. Elsa was taller than Kira. In fact, she was as tall as me, which kind of freaked me out at first because I tend to be taller than most people my age. She had a totally different look from Kira. Little makeup and not one piece of torn clothing.

"Hey," I said.

"So, listen," Kira said. "Let's go. There's this guy who has been watching me all night and it's getting creepy."

"Which one?" Riley said, as if he had been called upon to defend her honor.

"It doesn't matter. Just this guy. Come on."

We started walking back down the beach. Riley had the soccer ball beneath one arm. Kira was talking an endless stream, but Elsa and I were just far enough away that we couldn't clearly make out what she was saying.

"So, how do you know Kira?" Elsa finally asked.

"I don't. I mean, I just met her now."

"Oh." This ended our first conversation. We listened to the noise of Kira talking for a few minutes before I came up with, "It's a nice night out."

"Yeah. Warm. But not too hot." We both nodded in agreement to this statement. It was indeed warm but not too hot.

So you get the general idea of exactly how smooth I am with girls.

Kira gave Riley a shove, and he dropped the soccer ball. I darted down the beach and flicked it up into my hand before it rolled into the waves.

"Wow, fast," Kira said. "Do you play?"

"Soccer?" I asked.

"Obviously."

"Yeah," I said, then pointed at Riley. "We both do."

"What position?" Elsa asked.

"Striker."

"Defense," Riley said.

"We play too," Kira said.

"Yeah?"

"Both of us are midfield, but I sometimes play defense," Elsa said.

"So you are the guys Del flies by, then," Riley said.

"Um, I doubt it," Kira said. "Our team is number one."

"Which school?" I asked.

"We don't play on the school team. Our school team sucks. We play for the Furies."

"Impressive," Riley said. "But I still bet Del would blow right past you. He's pretty much the best player on our team. In fact, there's a scout coming next week to check him out."

"A scout. Wow, impressive," Elsa said.

"How much do you want to bet?" Kira said, taking the ball.

"Bet what?" Riley said.

"Ice cream," Elsa said. "I want some ice cream."

"What?" I said. These girls were confusing. It was obvious they spent a lot of time together.

"Del gets five goals on us and we buy the ice cream," Kira said. "We stop him five times, you guys buy."

"And what am I supposed to do while all this is going on?" Riley asked.

Kira grabbed his arm. "You're keeper."

"I am a horrible keeper," Riley said.

"Well, you'd better get good fast."

We went to this crappy field Angelo had in the lot next to his restaurant. It was a community field that Romano's dad had put together, then immediately abandoned. As we passed by the restaurant, I saw that Romano's car was still in the parking lot.

There were people inside too, but the lights had been dimmed and I couldn't tell who any of them were.

The field was all chewed up, and the goals didn't have nets. But that's the beauty of soccer—you really don't need anything other than a ball.

Riley set himself up as goalkeeper.

"Hey, wait a minute. Why would I try and stop anything if in the end I just have to buy you two ice cream?"

"Because," Kira said.

"Because why?" Riley yelled back.

"Just because." The field wasn't lit, but the streetlights cast enough of a glow for us to see.

I set the ball at center field and put my foot on it.

"So, five goals?"

"Yeah," Elsa said. "But you have to get around both of us before shooting. No trying to just flip it in or blast one."

"Okay," I said. "And what counts as you stopping me?"

Elsa and Kira looked at one another.

"The ball going behind you," Kira said.

"All right." I looked at the ball, then at the girls. Everything was a little hazy in the half-light. "Can I go?"

"No, wait," Kira said. She took a few steps toward me, then began running. "Now you can go," she yelled, when she was a few feet away. I rolled the ball to one side and flicked it over her foot. She went flying right past me. I started up the field. Elsa was moving sideways, trying to block me off.

"Take left!" she yelled to Kira. I went straight down the right line, then stopped just short of where Elsa was and darted toward center. Elsa slid and started laughing as I rolled past Kira again and shot the ball between the posts. Riley didn't even try to stop it.

"Riley!" Kira yelled.

"Sorry, I didn't see him coming."

Elsa ran up beside me and said, "You *are* good." Riley hoofed the ball back out to center and we started over again. This time, both girls came straight at me. I tried to move to the left but looked up into Elsa's smiling face and got kind of distracted. She kicked the ball away, sending it to roll over center field.

"Nice!" Kira yelled. They high-fived one another.

"One-one, sucker," Elsa said.

"All right, all right," I said. I took the ball back and waited to start again.

"Hey, guys," Riley yelled. "I forgot my backpack in Angelo's. I'm going to run in before it closes." There was a line of trees and a giant hedge separating Angelo's from the field. Riley darted between two of the trees and disappeared into the hedge.

"You lost your keeper," I said.

"That's all right—he sucked anyway," Kira replied. "Bring it on."

I pretended to hesitate and then drove quickly out to the left line. The girls scrambled but were on me fast. I stopped up short and felt Elsa's hands grab at my arm. Kira was kicking away at the ball beneath me. I rotated back around Elsa, and she grabbed on to my arm and tugged me sideways.

"Hey, that's a foul."

"Not in this league," Elsa said. I managed to keep the ball away from Kira and yanked my arm away from Elsa at the same time. Then I started running toward the goal. Kira fell as she started after me.

"Get him, El!" she yelled. "Take no prisoners!"

I slowed up a little, though I didn't need to. Elsa was really fast, and soon enough she was tapping the ball from beneath me. She spun around and kicked it, but it just bounced off my shins and rolled away from us. We both ran for the ball and, at the same time, grabbed one another's arms.

"Come on, El!" Kira yelled again. She was up and brushing herself off. Elsa kept laughing.

"No. Way. You. Are. Getting. This. Ball," she said.

"I so am."

"You are so not." We spun around again, still holding on to one another. Then Elsa's grip slipped and we were holding hands, doing a kind of awkward dance around the ball. I rolled it slightly

Jeff Ross

to the left, and she kicked it hard. Kira scrambled after it and kicked it away. As I went to let go of Elsa's hand, she squeezed mine once, then again, before letting go.

"Told you you wouldn't get that ball," she said.

"Next one's mine," I said as I started running toward center field. I had gotten about halfway when we heard a car tearing down the street followed by Riley screaming for help.

chapter six

We ran through the trees and into the restaurant's parking lot. We couldn't see Riley at first. We could just hear him screaming "help" over and over again. We found him down beside the driver's-side door of Romano's car.

"Call an ambulance or something," Riley said. "Someone took Romano out."

"What?" I said. Elsa already had her phone out and was dialing. It was then that I spotted Romano on the ground.

"I just found him here. The front door of the restaurant was locked, so I went around back to get in. But the back door was locked too, so I came back and here he was."

"Who would have done this?" I said. I was frozen.

"I saw a car take off right after I found him. It was an old black muscle car. Tell the police that."

Elsa was talking into her cell. "Police—I don't know, ambulance too? There's been an attack."

I finally got a grip on myself and went down on one knee beside Romano. He was completely out. For some reason I put my hand on his forehead, as if I were checking to see if he had a fever. He instantly startled and sat up straight, his eyes shooting open.

"What?" he gasped.

"You're all right," Riley said, grabbing him by both shoulders. "It's cool."

Romano reached out and grabbed at his ankle. "Ahh, what the hell happened?"

I looked at his ankle. It was bulging, and his sock was bloody.

"I just found you here," Riley said. "Do you remember anything?"

"Someone came up behind me while I was getting into my car and choked me out."

Riley said, "Who would do that?"

"I don't know," Romano said. "I didn't see him."

The door to the restaurant opened and Angelo came running out. "Romano, what happened?"

We dealt with the police, answering the same questions over and over again. "What did you see?"

"Nothing."

"What did you hear?"

"A car peeling out."

"Who could have done this?"

To which we had no answer. Not then anyway. It seemed totally random. But then, it couldn't be. That kind of thing just doesn't happen in Resurrection Falls.

The next morning, Saturday, we were all seated in the locker room, examining Romano's busted ankle. Maybe not busted, but messed up in countless ways. Whatever he'd been hit with had cut deeply into his skin. Romano was going back to the hospital that afternoon for another X-ray. But no matter what happened, he would not be playing any more soccer that year.

"That is bullshit," Jared said. "Man, I should have stuck around longer."

"No one expected someone to take me out in the parking lot of my father's restaurant," Romano said.

"Yeah, but we had to know those Roland Hills asshats would retaliate. Damn it, I should have stayed, man." Jared was really getting worked up about it.

"We don't know that it was them," Oz said.

"No? Who then?" Jared demanded. "Who?"

Coach came into the room with a mug of coffee steaming away in one hand. "All right, lads, let's all take a seat," he said.

He walked over to Romano and put a hand on his shoulder. "I was sorry to hear about what happened. How are you?"

"Shitty," Romano said.

"I understand that the police have opened a full investigation," Coach said. He looked at the rest of us. "So we'll let them do their job. Okay? Our job is to get back on the pitch and play hard." He squeezed Romano's shoulder. "We need to do it for Romano here."

"It was Doug Richards," Jared said. "I know it. He even owns one of those stupid muscle cars."

"Who?" Riley said.

"It doesn't matter," Coach interrupted. "If this young man had anything to do with the attack, he will most certainly be caught and brought to justice." He let go of Romano's shoulder and turned to address us. "I don't want any of you to get involved with this. We suffered a disappointment yesterday. But I believe that when you fall down, you get right back up. That's why we're here today. With Romano gone, we're down to one substitute. The rules state that once the playoffs begin, no team is allowed to add any new players. I've put a call in this morning to see if there might be a way for us to work around this rule and bring a new player in."

"Who?" Oz asked.

"I don't know. I suppose we'll have to bring someone up from the junior team. But as it stands at the moment, you will all be playing each and every minute of every match. That will be a challenge, and it doesn't leave any room for injuries. So, I want you to get out there and practice today. Practice hard but smart. I don't want anyone else getting hurt. Understood?"

There was a grumble of agreement in the room.

"The first round has been set. We start on Monday against Central West. I know we beat Central West by a fair margin during the season."

"Seven to nothing, right?" Oz said.

"Right, exactly. But I don't want any of you to take this team lightly. We need to play them hard. We need to show that we have the intensity and winning spirit necessary to go all the way. We're not just playing Central West on Monday, we're sending a message to all of the teams that we are winners. That we are the best team."

"Damn straight!" Jared said.

"So, play hard, play smart, play to win. Let's get out there." Everyone jumped up and started for the door. "Riley, Del, Romano, could you hang back a moment?"

The rest of the team streamed out the door. Coach took a long pull on his coffee, then said, "What happened last night, lads?" Romano and Riley went through the story again.

Coach looked at me. "What did you see, Del?"

"Nothing," I said.

"Did any of you see this Doug Richards kid last night at all?"

"No," Romano said. "But everyone knows my father owns the restaurant and that we all hang out there after games. He could have just been waiting for me to come out."

"Right. Well." Coach slapped a hand on Romano's shoulder again. "Let it die there, all right? What's done is done."

Romano nodded.

"I'm sorry you won't be able to play. We really could have used you. But know that whatever victories we enjoy now are in large part because of you. You've played hard all year."

"Thanks, Coach," Romano said.

"Are you going to stay and watch practice?"

"I have to go see a specialist." Romano stumbled forward on his crutches. "But I'll be at the game on Tuesday."

"Of course you will," Coach said. "We'll have you on the bench."

"Thanks, Coach," Romano said as he hobbled out of the room.

Coach took another long pull on his coffee while staring at the far wall. "You two really didn't see anything?"

"No. I wish I had," Riley said. "Just the car taking off and Rom on the ground." They both looked at me.

"I was on the other side of the trees. So I didn't see anything either."

"What about this car? Did you hear it too?"

I thought back. There had been a noise right before Riley yelled. It could have been a car taking off. "I might have heard a car leaving the parking lot. I don't know for sure."

"It was a black muscle car. I know Doug Richards has one."

Coach nodded. "Well, like I said, the police will investigate. You two keep your mind on the upcoming games. It's not going to be easy."

"Will do, Coach," Riley replied.

We ran drills for three hours that morning. It was excruciating and hot, and everyone seemed a little down. I have to admit, I wasn't really paying that much attention to practice. Because after all the police and paramedics and everything had finished the night before, I'd walked Elsa to the bus stop. We'd sat and talked for a while, and by the time her bus finally came, we had agreed to meet up the next afternoon.

So as much as I loved shooting penalty shots and running endless laps around the track, I was already seeing myself with Elsa again. On a date.

chapter seven

Elsa was waiting outside the coffee shop where we had agreed to meet. She had one foot against the wall and was reading a book. I was mildly freaked out again by her height. She was taller than any girl my age I'd ever met.

"Hey," I said.

"Oh, hey," she replied, dropping the book to her side.

"What are you reading?" She held the cover toward me. It read *That Summer*. "Is it good?"

"I don't know yet. I just started it. My sister gave it to me because I'm tall." I must have looked at her strangely. "It's about a tall girl."

"Oh, okay," I said. Then, again because I am super suave, "You are tall."

"Yeah, tell me about it."

"Does it bother you?" She raised an eyebrow at me. "I mean, not that it should or anything, but..."

"No, because I'm supermodel-tall, right?"

"Really?"

"Really what?"

"What is supermodel-tall?"

"It was a joke. Because supermodels are usually tall," she said.

Man, am I smooth, I thought. "Oh, yeah. For sure," I said. "You want to go inside?"

She looked through the window of the coffee shop. "Not really."

"Oh, okay. What do you want to do?" I said, already feeling off balance. I'd had a whole plan for how to sit, what to order, how to go about paying for Elsa without it seeming weird.

"You want to go for a drive in the hills?"

"You have a car?"

"I have something to drive. Just my mother's crappy minivan though."

"Hey, wheels are wheels, right?"

"Maybe," she said.

"The hills" were the ski hills that sat to the west of Resurrection Falls. They weren't huge or anything. In fact, you could drive to the top of all of them. And, I imagine, you could drive a Jeep down any number of them as well. But they were good enough for some snowboarding or, from what I'd heard, skateboarding down the steep main road.

"I never do this," I said as we turned onto Beacon Hill Road.

"Drive around?"

"Well, I guess sometimes. But never up here."

"I do," Elsa said.

"Why?"

"You'll see," she said.

We talked about soccer and school and what had happened to Romano the night before, and how strange it had all been.

"How is he doing?" she asked.

"I guess all right. He was going for another X-ray today."

"Do they have any idea who did it to him?"

"Not really. Riley said he saw this car that he thought belonged to this guy from—"

"Wait. Okay, here it is." Elsa turned down a lane that I hadn't even seen.

"Where are we going?" I said.

She reached over and patted my knee. "You'll see."

We drove along the rutted path, tree branches slapping at the windshield, until we came to a parking lot of sorts.

"What's this for?" I said.

"Cross-country skiing. The road is actually way better maintained in the winter." We got out, and I followed Elsa to a path through the trees.

"Now where are we going?"

"You'll see," she said again. "Patience, patience."

"This is starting to feel like a bad horror movie. Only reversed," I said as I dodged a swinging branch.

"What do you mean by reversed?"

"Well, normally it's some creepy guy luring a beautiful girl into the woods."

"You're not creepy," she said. Then she turned and punched me on the arm. "Though you got the rest right." She grabbed my hand and dragged me through an opening in the trees. We were just above the top of a ski lift. The chairs were all rocking slightly in the breeze.

"Don't they take these down in the summer?" I said.

"This lift hasn't run in years. So I guess they just leave the chairs where they are."

She jammed her foot against the side of the lift cabin and jumped up into the chair.

"There we go," she said. "Come on up." She shifted on the chair so that I could hop up beside her.

"And this is why I brought you all the way up here."

The view was amazing. Resurrection Falls lay beneath us. The sky was a pure blue, dotted by a few lazy clouds.

"Wow," I said.

"Yeah, that's called perspective," Elsa said. "It's why I come up here."

"What do you mean?"

"I mean, I get pretty caught up in things. Like school and soccer and everything. And it's hard to just breathe and let it go down there. So I end up feeling as if I'm getting angry all the time for no reason. That's when I come up here and look at this."

"You get angry?"

"Yeah, Del, everyone gets angry. But think about it." She reached up and brought the safety bar down, then leaned on it.

"This is one little town in a country of little towns and giant cities. And our country is just one country out of a whole bunch of other countries."

"Yeah," I said. "It's a big world." Which sounded totally lame.

She fell silent for a moment. "What I'm saying is that when I'm up here, all the things that piss me off down there seem pretty small."

"Do you come up here a lot?"

"No, I'm only a little dysfunctional." I stared at her and she laughed. "Everyone is though, right?"

"Absolutely," I said. I could see Angelo's restaurant and the soccer field beside it. "You know, maybe whoever took Romano out should come up here sometime."

"Right, we were talking about that before. Do the police have any idea who did it?"

"Maybe. Riley saw a car tear off, and he thinks it belongs to this guy Doug Richards."

"Doug Richards who goes to Roland Hills?"

"Yeah. Do you know him?"

Elsa looked dead at me. "Yeah, I know him. He's my brother's best friend."

chapter eight

When we got back to the van, Elsa grabbed her phone and started dialing her brother's number.

"Doug had nothing to do with it." She set the phone on the dash and put it on speaker.

"El, where are you? I've been trying to get a hold of you," her brother said.

"I'm out. What's going on with Doug?"

"The police were just here. Something happened last night to that kid who took

Tim Irvine out, and they think Doug had something to do with it."

"I know, I was there," Elsa said. "But it wasn't Doug, right?" There was a long silence. "Evan, right?"

"I don't—I mean, no. He couldn't have. Wait, what were you doing there?"

She looked at me. "Where was Doug last night?"

"El, I don't know. I mean, you can't tell anyone this, but I told the police he was with me."

"But he wasn't?"

"No, not when the thing happened he wasn't. He was earlier, but we'd split up by then."

"So you lied to the police?" Elsa said.

"Not really. I mean, we had been together. And anyway, Doug couldn't have done it. It's just not possible."

Elsa looked at me again. I didn't know what to say. Actually, I didn't want to say anything, because then her brother would know I was there.

"Listen, El, come home. We need to talk about this. What were you even doing there last night?"

"I was out with Kira," she said. I was getting the sense that this family didn't have issues with telling half-truths. "I'll be home in half an hour."

"I'll be here."

Elsa ended the call and dropped her phone into a drink holder.

"So..."

"He didn't do it, Del. There's no way. You don't know Doug. He just wouldn't—he couldn't. He's the nicest guy."

"Okay," I said, remembering how he had let his anger get the better of him when he attacked Romano.

"You can't tell anyone what you just heard. Promise." I didn't know what to say. This was exactly the kind of information the police needed. "At least, not until this is all figured out. You have to promise." She put a hand on my arm, and I looked into her big green eyes.

"Sure, I mean, yeah. I won't say anything."

Elsa started the van and drove back out to Beacon Hill Road. "He's the nicest guy," she said again. Even then, it seemed as if she was trying to convince herself of the fact.

I texted Riley on our way back into town. The team was gathering at Angelo's. This whole situation was seriously confusing. First off, I had had no idea that Elsa went to Roland Hills. Add this to the fact that the guy we suspected of taking out one of our teammates was a good friend of hers, and honestly, I didn't have a clue where I stood.

The restaurant was packed with people. It was as if the entire community had come together to support Romano's family after the attack. There were get-well cards everywhere, and the tip jar was stuffed to overflowing. Rom was propped up in a booth, his cast-enclosed leg on full display.

Jared, Oz and Riley were on the other side of the booth. There were greasy paper plates and half-finished glasses of soft drinks on the table.

"Hey, guys," I said, standing beside the table.

"I suppose you want me to move my leg, right?" Rom said.

"No, that's cool." I grabbed a chair and sat down at the end of the table. "What's going on?"

"We've been talking about the situation," Jared said.

"What situation?" I said.

"The situation that has me bench surfing for the entire playoffs," Rom said.

"Of course," I said. "Yeah."

"We're trying to figure out how to strike back," Oz said.

"What do you mean?" Jared sat up straight at the end of the booth.

"We don't think it was that Doug Richards prick anymore."

"Yeah, he talked to the police and he has an alibi," Oz said.

"How do you know?" I asked.

"My friend Devon's dad is a cop. He was the one who questioned Doug and then confirmed the alibi."

"So it wasn't him," Jared said. "Which means it had to be one of the other pricks on the team."

"Unless he was lying," I said without thinking.

"Who?" Oz said. "You mean Doug?"

"Yeah," I said. "People lie to the police all the time."

Jared leaned forward on the table. "Did you hear something?"

I didn't want to give Elsa up. I noticed that Riley was looking away from me. I guessed that he, too, had discovered which school the girls went to. Or maybe he'd known all along.

"Yeah, kind of," I said.

"From who?" Oz said.

"I don't really want to say, you know?"

"Doesn't matter," Jared said. "Was the information good? Do you trust this person?"

"Yeah," I said. "I do." And I did. But even as I was saying it, I realized that within ten minutes of promising I wouldn't say a word to anyone, I had broken Elsa's trust.

"What did you hear?"

"I don't know," I said. But I was already in too deep. "Just that Doug Richards might not have been where he said he was. That's all. And that his alibi might not be one hundred percent solid."

"The prick," Oz said. "This means he did it. Why else would he lie?"

I said, "I'm not defending the guy or anything, but it just means that he wasn't where he said he was."

"That was his car," Riley muttered.

"What?" Jared said. He was getting red in the face.

"That was his car," Riley said. "I know it."

"The prick," Jared said again.

"We don't know," I said.

"Well," Riley said, "I know how we can find out."

"How?"

"I know where Doug Richards will be tonight. We can go ask him."

Oz and Jared laughed. "Just walk up and ask?" Oz said. "Sounds perfect."

"No," Jared said, giving Riley a slap on the back. "There's asking, and then there's *asking*. Where will he be tonight?"

"The abandoned mall out on Route Four."

"Why would anyone go there?" Oz said.

"Apparently, his friends hang out there. They like to explore, I guess."

"Okay, then," Jared said, nodding. "We'll go exploring tonight too."

chapter nine

The Westmount Mall closed its doors back in 2010. For a while there was talk of rejuvenating the place and making it into an outlet mall. But the talk never turned into action, and now it's just a place for kids to run around inside and trash things.

Most of the doors are boarded up, but plywood is defenseless against curious teen-agers. We were at one of the side entrances. There were footprints in the dust, and one of the pieces of plywood covering the door looked warped and weak.

"What about security?" I said as Jared pulled the board to one side.

"What security?"

"There has to be security here, right?" I said.

"Not anymore," Oz said, laughing. "The only thing we have to worry about is some gang hanging out in here."

"What gang?" Riley said, laughing.

"I just heard that there's a gang that decided to make this their headquarters or something." Oz ducked in after Jared, leaving Riley and me standing outside.

"You first," Riley said.

"No, you. I insist."

"Fine." Riley ducked in and disappeared.

I followed. Inside, it was dark and smelled of urine and smoke.

"Where will they be?" Jared whispered.

"I don't know. I just heard they come here," Riley said.

"Who'd you hear that from?" Jared said. "It could be a setup."

Riley flicked on his flashlight. When he didn't answer, I knew exactly who had told him Doug would be in this place—Kira.

"This is creepy," Oz said. "How many of them do you think there'll be?"

"Doesn't matter," Riley said. "We're just here to talk, right?" We all turned our flashlights on. The beams tracked along closed stores. Some of them had security gates or sliding doors. Most were just giant holes. My mother used to bring me here for shoes and school clothes. I would try to convince her to buy me a pair of skater shoes, but I always ended up with some run-of-the-mill white or red trainers.

"How are we supposed to find anyone in here?" Oz said.

"Let's just look around," Jared replied. "If we don't find them, it's still pretty cool in here."

"Not really," I said.

"Grow a pair, Del," Jared said. He kicked at some broken glass. The noise rang through the empty corridors.

Everything went completely silent after the echoing stopped. Then we heard something like footsteps coming from the corridor to our right. Jared held a finger to his lips. He pointed at Oz, then at a closed-down magazine shop on the left. He shut his flashlight off, and the corridor went dark again. He leaned in close to me and said, "You and Riley move up to the corner, then run as fast as you can up this hallway. If anyone follows you, I'll take them down."

"Okay," I said. Three flashlight beams cut through the darkness ahead of us. "But I thought we were just here to talk."

"Sure, sure," Jared said. "But we still want the upper hand in the conversation, right?" He patted me on the back. I whispered the plan to Riley. Then we moved to the corner.

There was just enough moonlight coming in through the skylights to make out the corridor. I put a hand on Riley's back, then let go as I took off running. Riley was right behind me. There was motion to our right. I didn't turn to see who or what had emerged from the other corridor. We jumped over a bench and slid to a stop. There was a crash, and then someone yelled.

"What the hell!" Riley grabbed my arm and pulled me to one side. I turned around to find Jared sitting on top of Doug Richards. Oz was beside him. Two other guys I recognized from the Rebels team were closing in. Everyone had their flashlights pointed at one another as if they were guns and this was the end of some badass Tarantino movie.

"We have them outnumbered," Riley said. "Anything happens and it's you and me, all right?" I really, really didn't want anything to happen. I wasn't much for violence. I'd never even punched anyone before, and I wasn't looking to start just then.

"Doug Richards," Jared said.

"Get off me," Doug replied.

"I just have a couple of questions," Jared said. One of Doug's friends came over and shoved Jared. He flew forward, and Doug scrambled back to his feet.

"What the hell are you doing?" Doug said. He had a cut on his cheek. He wiped at it, then stared at his hand.

"What happened, Richards?" Jared said. "Tell us where you were when Romano was taken out."

"Nowhere near him, you asshat."

"Then why was your car seen tearing away from the scene?"

Doug was regaining some of his composure. Up to that point, it had seemed as if he could cry at any moment. "I was nowhere near that idiot's restaurant."

"Oh, so you know where it happened, then?" Jared said.

"Yeah, I know. The police have already been to visit me because of something someone told them. Something that was utter bullshit."

"Where were you, Richards?" Jared said. "That's all we're asking."

"Not there." Doug pulled the tail of his shirt up to his forehead and dabbed at the cut.

"Prove it," Jared said.

"I was with Evan," Doug said. Evan, Elsa's brother, took a little step forward. I could see the resemblance. Though Evan was shorter than Elsa, he was way more thick and muscular. He was wearing a hoodie and, for some reason, a pair of winter gloves.

"That's bullshit," Jared said. "We already know it. Where were you really?"

"What do you know?" Evan said.

To Jared's credit, he did not give me up. "We know. And the police will know soon too." Jared took a step toward Doug. Jared was a lot bigger than Doug, and he looked really pumped up by the situation.

"You don't have any proof," Evan said.

"How do you know we don't have any proof?" Jared said.

"Because we have—" Evan began.

"Shut up," Doug interrupted.

"What do you have?" Jared asked.

I felt Riley tense up beside me. "Del," he said.

"What?" Then I saw it too. Three large, bright beams of light were tracking the wall behind Doug and his crew.

Someone yelled, "Hey, what's going on down here?"

Jared shone his light down the corridor. I didn't know who the guys were because their flashlights were so bright. But there were at least three of them. Whether they had any reason to be in the mall or not, we definitely didn't.

One of them yelled something, but I had no idea what. Before he'd even finished the sentence, we were all running as fast as humanly possible.

chapter ten

One set of lights lit up Doug and his group, while another came up behind us. Going out the way we'd come in wasn't an option. Not that anyone was thinking strategically. We all just started running whichever way we were facing.

Someone behind me yelled, "Got one!" and I briefly wondered who it was that'd been caught.

"Run, Del," Riley said. He was right beside me.

"Where?" I yelled. He didn't respond. We were in an every-man-for-himself situation.

I could vaguely recall the layout of the mall. There were two corridors I remembered getting lost in as a kid, one up on the left, the other around the corner, on the other side of the square. They both had restrooms, but only one had doors to the outside.

The problem was, I couldn't remember which was which.

Someone was right behind us, his flashlight beam reflecting off the walls, throwing our shadows on empty storefronts. I tried to make out the right corridor, hoping it hadn't been boarded up. Hoping that the door at the end wasn't chained shut or something.

"This way," I yelled at Riley, but he'd stopped listening. He was rounding the corner, heading toward the square. I was certain the corridor on the left was the one with the door at the end.

I swung into it, my footsteps echoing loudly. I could hear people yelling, and something smashed.

At first it seemed as if our pursuer had followed Riley. But then the bright beam lit up the corridor and someone yelled, "Stop right there."

I passed the women's restroom, then a set of lockers, a water fountain and finally the men's restroom. The end of the corridor was too far away for me to see whether there was a door or not. I just kept running, feeling my heart beating hard in my chest.

Whoever was following me had stopped running. As the end of the corridor came into focus, I realized why.

In front of me was a wall. I was in the wrong corridor. I turned back around.

"Got you, kid," the guy said. "What are you doing in here? Don't you know this is our place?"

I darted back to the men's restroom.

The moon shone through a set of high windows, making it a little brighter inside. There was junk all over the floor. Empty boxes and bits of pipe. I had to make a quick decision. It would be possible to climb up on the end cubicle and get to the ledge that ran along the base of the windows, but I had no idea what was on the other side.

Instead, I grabbed the largest pipe I could find and threw it as hard as I could. One of the windows smashed. I ducked into a cubicle and jumped onto the toilet seat just as the restroom door opened.

"What the hell?" the guy said. "You didn't just seriously..." I froze. Tried not to breathe. I heard the guy pulling himself up onto the frame of the final cubicle. I dared to take a quick look. He was wearing a baseball cap and holding a giant flashlight in one hand.

I waited for him to get fully up on the ledge beneath the windows. Then I slid off the toilet and opened the cubicle door. The hinges heaved and screeched, and the guy spun around so fast, I thought he was going to fall off the ledge.

"There you are!" he said. I bolted out the restroom door and back into the corridor.

There were lights all over the place farther down the main corridor. I could see people slipping on the floor. Flashes of legs and arms spinning wildly.

I hit the end of the corridor going full speed and turned to the right, hoping I could still get out where we'd come in. But when I was halfway down the corridor, two bright beams lit me up and someone yelled, "There's one of them!"

I slid under the accordion doors of what was once a comic-book store. I remembered visiting this place in the past. The giant boxes of old comics on a table down the middle of the store and racks of new ones climbing each wall. The glass case beneath the counter with Magic and Pokémon cards inside. But, more important, the back room, which was home to both a tiny, cell-like bathroom and an outside door.

I tripped over something in the dark, almost losing my flashlight. There was garbage everywhere. Turned-over shelves and broken glass.

The accordion door banged behind me.

"Get out here, you little shit," someone said. I shone my light at the back of the store, then turned it off and scrambled to my feet. "You're trapped in here, kid."

I banged my shin on something and almost wiped out again, hands just grazing the floor. Something sliced into my palm, but I barely noticed. I threw myself into the back of the store and, luckily, found the tiny hallway with the bathroom on one side and the door to a loading dock on the other.

I turned sideways and put all my weight into the door, making certain to hit the security bar with my hip.

The door popped open and I was out on a loading dock. I jumped to the ground and took off through the empty parking lot.

"Get back here!" someone yelled. I chanced a look back. There were two guys standing on the loading dock, their flashlights trained on me. There was a big sprawl of graffiti on the wall behind them. I turned back around and ran as fast as I could.

Luckily, we had parked Jared's car on a nearby street. I could see someone leaning against the hood. As I got closer, I realized it was Riley.

"Holy crap," I said, completely out of breath. "What the hell was that?"

"That was crazy. Did you see Jared or Oz?"

"No. I just kept running. How did you get out?"

"Are you kidding me? I used to spend hours in that place. It was like my mom's idea of babysitting. Stay in the mall. Don't leave with anyone. Don't go outside. I'll come find you in an hour."

"Seriously? Your mom did that?"

Riley shrugged. "She didn't always have a choice. She worked at the shoe store. I used to come out here after school and just walk the halls."

"Oh," I said, grabbing my knees and trying to slow my breathing.

"So I know all the exits."

"Any idea who those guys were?"

"Oz was talking about that gang who made this their hangout," Riley said. We heard pounding feet in the darkness. I prepared myself to run.

"Oz, Jared," Riley said.

"Get in the car," Jared said, darting past us and unlocking the doors. "Come on. I don't know if we shook them or not." Riley and I jumped into the back seat as Jared got the car started.

"What the hell was that?" Riley said.

Jared did a quick one-eighty and gunned it up the street.

"I have no idea," Oz said. "But I wasn't going to stick around and find out."

As we turned toward the highway, three guys with giant flashlights came running out of the mall parking lot.

"That was them," Oz said. One of them threw something at the car. Jared stepped on the gas, and we roared down the street.

"Those weren't security guards," Riley said. "No way."

I looked at my hand. There was a small cut along my palm. It was dripping blood all over my pants. I looked through the back window at the guys who'd chased us. They turned back toward the mall, and I wondered whether Doug and his friends, especially Elsa's brother, had gotten out.

chapter eleven

Monday, after school, Coach arrived in the locker room five minutes earlier than he normally did. We were playing the seventh-place team in the first round of the playoffs. During the regular season, we'd destroyed them 6-1. But this was elimination time, and it seemed, year after year, that anything could happen.

"We're in the final stretch, lads," Coach said. "We had a misstep. But don't think for a moment that the championship is not still firmly within our grasp. We need to look at this one game at a time. We need to win today. And to do that, we need to play our best soccer yet." He seemed strangely calm for the occasion. "Now, with the loss of Romano, we are without any subs. But I spoke with the league and they have allowed us to add a player who was not on the team during the regular season. However, we are unable to bring up one of our junior players due to age requirements. Luckily, we have a perfectly fine substitute who just happens to be a senior."

A guy I'd seen around came into the locker room.

"This is Jean. He is originally from a suburb of Paris, am I correct, Jean?"

Jean nodded. He was thin and tall, with a curly mop of black hair.

"Jean played on his high school team over in France." Coach put his hand on Jean's shoulder. "What position did you play there?"

"Defense," Jean said.

"That should work," Coach said. "We'll get you in right away, then. Dan, you can start the game out. We'll keep you rested and get you in for the second half." Coach clapped his hands. "All right, lads, let's get out there and win, win, win."

We were the first team on the field, which had never happened before. I didn't know whether this shifting of tactics was yet another mind game from Coach or if he had finally changed his ways.

"Welcome, boys," the ref said. It was the same guy who had kicked Romano out and, in the minds of many of our players, lost the game for us by awarding a penalty kick. "I see we're timely today."

"Do we get to flip the coin without the other team out here?" Jared said. "You know, decide on heads or tails once it hits the ground?"

"That would never happen," the ref said.

The other team came out between the bleachers. A few of its supporters were in the crowd—though, again, "crowd" was a bit of an overstatement. It was a drizzly, gray day, and only the most die-hard fans were in attendance. As I ran to my striker position, I noticed someone waving from the bleachers. Huddled there in a blue raincoat was Kira, waving like crazy and hollering at us. Elsa was beside her. She wasn't waving or yelling. Even though I didn't know her *that* well, she seemed angry.

"All right, guys, let's do this!" Jared yelled. The ref blew his whistle and Jared kicked the ball directly to me. There was immediate pressure from the other team as its striker and right midfielder charged. I kicked the ball back to one of our midfielders and sprinted forward as the other team began double- or triple-teaming whoever had the ball. If this was their strategy, it wasn't going to work unless they had a neverending supply of subs on the bench. You have to conserve energy in soccer whenever possible, and running around like the field is on fire is not going to do it.

Our team began cycling the ball, moving it forward and back. We were in no rush.

With the other team wasting energy, it would be easy enough to eventually find a seam and move the ball upfield.

I have found that when playing a team intent on furiously chasing the ball down, one of the best techniques is just to stand still. You might have a defender kind of hovering around you for a bit, but eventually he'll get bored and cut to wherever the action is. So for a while, I simply stayed onside and waited. It was almost like being a spectator. The other team was nuts about running the ball down. It was as if they'd never played us before. If our team has one clear strength over the other teams in the league, it's ball possession. We could play this kind of game forever.

Oz had the ball up the right side and was taking stuttering little steps, trying to shake off two defenders. I moved up along the left side of the field. Oz spun around, driving straight across the field. He spotted me there all by myself and sent the ball out ahead of me.

I ran as hard as I could, catching the ball with the inside of my foot just as it was about to dribble out of bounds. The keeper went wild, yelling at his defense to get back. But there was no way they would catch me. They'd overcommitted and were locked on the right side, trying to get around all the players moving upfield. I brought the ball in quickly, making certain I kept control. As I got closer, I sent the ball a little farther out in front of me. The keeper locked on. I faked a high corner kick, and he took the bait. He dove and I simply steered around him and lightly tapped the ball into the open net.

There were a couple of hoots from our side. Someone slapped me on the back. But we kept the celebration to a minimum. And with that goal, it seemed as if we'd drained all the energy the other team had brought onto the field. I was pretty sure they hadn't even touched the ball. Yet there they were, hands on knees, heads shaking, gulping water as they moved back upfield.

We scored two more goals during the first half. One came unexpectedly from Jean, who blocked a shot at our end, then ran the entire field in one swift motion, moving around the defending players as if they were pylons. The other came from Oz on a nice corner kick that bent right in past the keeper's outstretched arms.

At halftime, Riley and I went to the bleachers to talk with Kira and Elsa.

"You guys are awesome!" Kira said. She threw her arms around Riley's neck and kissed him full on the lips. I hadn't talked with Riley about Kira, but apparently the two of them had become much closer.

"Hey, Elsa," I said.

"We need to talk," she said.

"Okay. Like, after the game?"

"Yes. Right after the game." The whistle blew and we ran back to the field. I glanced back at Elsa once, but she wasn't even looking at me.

chapter twelve

We won the game 5-0. I was pulled partway through the second half to allow our one sub a bit of playing time. I honestly didn't mind. I was more concerned with what Elsa had to talk to me about than with the game. Plus, I'm not all that interested in humiliating other teams. Coach never specifically said that's what we should do, but he did tell us to "send a message." Once we'd won, there was maybe a little too much celebrating for my liking. A lot of high-fiving and yelling on the field as the other team slumped back to the locker room to change.

I ran over to Elsa as we left the field.

"I just need a shower. Where can we meet?"

"I have the van," she said. "We'll be in the parking lot." Kira and Riley were locked in an awkward-looking kiss. Kira looked like she wanted everyone to know she'd managed to snag some great catch. Riley seemed more concerned that people would notice this blatant PDA.

"Come on, Riley," I said, clapping him on the back. He let go of Kira and ran with me back to the change room.

"We pulled that one out nicely," Jared said. He was standing in the middle of the locker room with a towel wrapped around his waist.

"That was too easy, mon," Oz said. Then Romano came in on his crutches.

"Good game, guys," he said.

"That one was for you, man," Jared said. "That one and all the ones to come. They're for you, bro."

Coach came in smiling. "Good game, lads. One down, two to go. Jean, really nice game."

Jean had already taken his shirt off. He had looked tall and skinny before, but it was evident that he worked out. He had a six-pack like no one else in the room. His arms were thin but muscular. "Thank you," he said.

"I think we might move you up next game. Maybe midfield, or you could swap out with the strikers. Does that sound good?"

"Okay." There were some nervous glances around the room. We always talked about working as a team, but when it came right down to it, no one wanted to be shifted out of his position unless it meant the possibility of scoring more goals.

"We have another game tomorrow," Coach said. He patted Jared on the back, then silently left the room.

"Everyone who wants to can come to my dad's restaurant tonight," Romano said. "First round of pizzas on us."

"Nice," Jared said, putting an arm around Romano's shoulders. "We'll be there."

Riley and I found Elsa's van in the parking lot. Kira was talking on her cell phone and Elsa was sitting on the floor with her feet sticking out the side door.

"Hey," I said.

"Who'd you tell?" she asked as soon as Riley had gone around the van.

"What?"

"How did your friends know about Doug not being with my brother that night?" She wouldn't look directly at me. I didn't know what to tell her.

"I never said that you told me."

"But you told your friends what you heard from my brother," Elsa said.

"I just said I had heard that Doug might not have been where he'd told the police he was. That's all."

"But you wouldn't have known that if you hadn't been with me." She still hadn't looked at me. I didn't know what to do. I leaned against the side of the van.

"They were ready to go after someone else. I didn't figure anything would come of it."

"Well, something did."

"What?" I said.

"My brother got beat up the other night."

"At the mall?" I said before I could stop myself.

She finally looked up at me. "How did you know about that? Were you there?"

"It wasn't us. We just went there to talk. Then these other guys showed up. I think they might be a gang or something. Did one of them get your brother?"

"Yeah, one of them got my brother. And they think those guys were with you."

"No way! They chased us too. We thought they might be security guys at first, but..." Elsa was staring at me. "Is he okay?"

"What do you care?"

"Well, he's your brother and..."

"Yeah, but he's also your main competition, isn't he? What's your motto here?

Winning above all else? Isn't that what this team is all about?"

"The team, yeah, but not me," I said.

"What makes you so different?" She stood up and slammed the side door closed. She opened the driver's-side door and got in.

"Those guys who got your brother weren't with us. They chased us too. We were just lucky to get out of there."

"Sure, you were lucky," Elsa said. "And my brother wasn't." She turned and yelled out the other window, "Come on, Kira."

"What?" Kira said.

"Let's go."

"But we were just—"

"Let's go, Kira. Or you can stay here if you want. But I wouldn't."

"What's going on, El?" Kira said.

"We're leaving," Elsa said.

"Elsa," I said. "It's not how you think it is."

"No?" She inhaled deeply and closed her eyes. "You don't want to talk to me right now. Call me if you figure out how it *actually* is." She slammed her door closed.

I saw Kira give Riley one last kiss, then climb in and close her door.

We watched the van leave the parking lot and shoot through the stop sign.

"What just happened?" Riley said.

I didn't know what to tell him. I'd made a mess of things very quickly. "I don't know," I said.

"Women, right?" Riley slapped my back, then ran his sleeve along his lips. "That Kira sure does like to kiss a lot."

I laughed. "And you're complaining?"

"No. Not at all. Come on, let's go to Romano's and eat some of that crappy free pizza."

chapter thirteen

"We're going to figure out who did this, Rom," Jared was saying when we came into the restaurant. "It's about respect now. These guys are disrespecting us."

"I know," Rom said.

"It has to be that Doug Richards."

"He's one of their best players," Oz said.

"Exactly." Jared had been standing beside the booth. He swung into it and sat down heavily. Riley and I stood at the end of the table, looking down. "He's a senior, right?

This is his last year in high school. He hasn't had a championship. Man, that happens to you, you go through school coming *that close* to a championship and never getting it? It would eat at you."

"That doesn't mean he did it," I said.

Jared seemed to notice me for the first time. "Why are you defending this guy all the time?"

"I'm not," I said. "I'm just saying we should be certain we have the right guy, you know?"

Jared pounded his fist into his open palm. "It had to be him."

"So what are we going to do about it?" Oz said. "Coach said to drop it. He said if we did anything else, we'd be benched."

"There's not enough of us to bench anyone. And anyway, that's not what he said. He said if we *got caught* doing anything we'd be benched."

"Same thing," Oz said. He stood up and got out of the booth. "I'm out of here. I have other things to do. You all need to drop this."

"We don't retaliate and these guys will be laughing at us on the field. They'll own us before we even step out there."

"That's just in your head," Oz said. "We need to leave all of this on the field."

"We had," Jared said. "They brought it off the field."

"Whatever. Listen, I'm out. Don't tell me anything else. I don't want to hear about it." Oz moved around a couple of tables and was out the door. I heard the tinkling of the bell as he left, and it sent me back to the night of the attack.

I hadn't noticed the bells when we entered the restaurant. It had been too noisy. But I remembered hearing them ringing the night of the attack, when Elsa and Kira and I were playing soccer on the nearby field.

Riley slid into the seat beside Jared.

"I'm out too, Jare. It's not worth it," he said. "We get busted following these guys around or whatever, and we'll be off the team. There's too much at stake here."

"What's at stake, Riley?"

"Being on the team? Finishing this season as champions again? I've heard there's a scout coming to the next two games. One of the farm teams for the MLS."

Jared laughed. "What, and you think they're coming to watch you?" He glanced up at me. "We all know who the scouts are looking at."

"You never know, Jare."

"I know. I know exactly what's going on, Riley," Jared said, spitting Riley's name out. "And I know my place in all of this. I won't go on that field like a coward when we play those guys again. They think they own us, and they will. Don't you see?"

"No," Riley said. "I don't."

"Well, then, you never will." My phone vibrated in my pocket. I pulled it out and there was a text from Elsa. **You at the restaurant?** I texted back, **yes**. A second later my phone vibrated again. **Meet me beside the field next door. I'm already here**.

"I have to go," I said. Elsa had been so angry with me before that I seriously figured I'd never see her again.

"Where?" Jared asked. He raised an eyebrow at me.

"Just to meet up with someone. Don't worry about it."

"I'm not worried, man," he said. He put his fist out, and I gave it a quick bump. "No worries at all. Just be ready for the next game."

"I'll be ready."

I went outside quickly, the bell ringing above my head as I passed through the door.

Elsa was leaning against the side of her mother's van. It was dusk, and the sky was purple and orange above us.

"Hey," I said. "I didn't think you wanted to talk to me anymore."

"I was just angry," she said.

"Did you go for a perspective-sit on the mountain?"

She laughed. "I did," she said. "I was up there for over an hour." She pulled her cell phone out. "Which was when this came in." She held her phone up. I leaned in.

There were two people on the screen. One was a girl I had never seen before, the other was Doug Richards.

"Okay," I said.

Elsa turned the phone around. She tapped at it, then turned it back. "It's date and time stamped," she said.

I looked at the information. It was exactly the date and time when Romano had been attacked.

"That could be altered, I bet," I said.

"It was taken two blocks from here. They were at the ice-cream parlor. That's why Riley saw Doug's car." She put the phone in her pocket. I must have shaken my head or looked skeptical, because she immediately said, "You still think Doug did it?"

"Honestly, I don't even care anymore."

"Seriously? After all of this, you just don't care now?" she said.

"It's too much. And in the end, it doesn't matter. We got a sub and he's really good."

"Yeah, I heard about that."

"So it all turned out okay," I said. She did not look convinced. "Are you sure that picture is authentic?"

"Yes."

"How?"

"Because that girl Doug's with? That's my brother's girlfriend, Jackie. Or I guess I should say *was* my brother's girlfriend."

"Oh," I said. Then I realized what she was saying. "Doug was with her when Romano was attacked."

"Exactly."

"And that's why he didn't want to tell everyone where he was," I said.

"Exactly." She wiped at her face.

"Are you okay?" I said. I heard the bells above the door at the restaurant ring. A moment later Jared was on the sidewalk, heading in the other direction.

"No, not really. I thought she was a really nice girl. So did Evan. And Doug, well..."

"Yeah," I said. "Maybe he's not the great guy you thought he was." The bells rang again. Riley hit the sidewalk and looked our way first. I guess we were in enough shadow that he didn't see us standing there. He looked in the direction Jared had gone, then jacked his collar up around his face and kind of slumped off.

"What's that all about?" she asked.

"I don't know," I said. The bells had reminded me of something though. At first I wasn't sure *what* they'd reminded me of, but standing out by the field, the smell of wet grass in the air, it came back to me.

Riley had said the door to the restaurant was locked the night Romano was attacked. But I'd heard the bells ring twice that night. I was sure of it. One had to have been Romano coming out. But what about the other time? Was it someone going in?

Or someone coming out?

chapter fourteen

The next day, before Coach came into the locker room, I asked Riley where he had gone after he left the restaurant the night before.

"Home," he said. "Why?" When I'd last seen him, he had been heading in the opposite direction of his house. But I didn't want to bring this up. It would sound creepy, and then he'd have to explain why he'd just lied to me.

"Just wondering. Did you see Kira?"

"No, she's angry at me."

"Why?"

"Because I told her that maybe we're making out too much and I'd rather just talk now and then."

"What?" I said. "You just broke the cardinal rule of dating. What do you want to talk to her about?"

"I don't know—something. I don't feel like I even really know her. What about you and Elsa?"

"No epic make-out sessions on our part," I said. "But you never know what's around the corner, right?"

Coach came in then, and everyone quieted down. He stood there and looked at us for a moment. He has a twitch above his right eyebrow that flares up before games when he is anxious.

"Lads," he said. "Game two." There was something in the air. Something dense and tired. The team we were playing that day, the Wolverines, had taken us to extra time during the regular season. Oz had scored on a header just before the ref blew the whistle. It was that tight. The memory of this lingered.

"We had a tough go against these guys last time out." Everyone nodded. "The problem is that they don't have one style. And that is something we have to remember. We need to force them into playing *our* game. Not a game of their choosing. *Our* game. So we're going to keep control of the ball. We're going to win the 50/50s. We're going to play these guys hard. If they start rushing the ball, we slow things down. They try and slow things down, we put on the pressure. Whatever they want to do, we will not let them. Understand?"

"Yes, Coach," we said.

"I'm not going to be shouting from the sidelines either. Let them do the shouting. Let them think we're sunk. Let them try and beat us."

"Yes, Coach!" we said again.

"Let them think they have a bloody chance, lads." Without another word, he took a step back and opened the locker-room door.

We went out like soldiers on parade. One at a time. Our steps measured and slow.

After we crossed the road, Riley gave me a tap and pointed into the stands.

"That's the scout," he said.

"How do you know?"

"He was at another game. He's here to watch you."

"We don't know that." The crowd, which was larger than at the previous game even though the weather was worse, was clapping and shouting. What had been a drizzle before going into the locker room had turned into a downpour.

The Wolverines won the coin toss. The ref blew his whistle and their center quickly kicked the ball back to his midfielder. I remembered they had a solid defense. They kept four back, three in the mid and three up front. Our best offense was often to run the ball out of bounds and then try and get it deep with throw-ins or corner kicks. Going straight at these guys was almost impossible.

They moved the ball between their defenders. I decided to run up. I'm pretty fast and can sometimes dart in and snag a weak pass. But as soon as I ran in, they cycled the ball back up my side.

So this was the way they intended to play. They were going to try and get one or more of us deep and out of position, then run the field on the open side. It was a good plan, and it may have worked had Jean not been hovering around center. The pass went directly to the striker, but he lost control of it just long enough for Jean to step in, tap the ball to one side, deke to center and then back out to the line. He got around the midfielder in much the same way.

The problem with having four defenders is that it's more difficult to keep track of everyone. So while two of the defense players had moved up to intercept Jean, the other two had fallen back into the keeper's box. This kept me onside farther in than they should have allowed.

Jean let the defense come at him, then popped the ball up over their heads directly to me. I took the ball on my chest, rotated around it as it fell and managed a good sweeping kick directly on goal.

Their keeper caught it squarely. He waved at his players to head upfield, but we'd accomplished something we had never really set out to. Everyone was wary of Jean. They hadn't seen him play before. But now they knew the kind of weapon he could be.

The defensive players were clapping in that way people do to get adrenaline flowing again and yelling, "Come on, come on!"

The rain was brutal. Guys were falling all over the place. As soon as you picked up speed, you began to slip and slide. Weather usually isn't a huge factor in soccer. Sometimes it's too hot and people get overheated or it's too cold and all their energy gets sapped. But the rain normally just adds a slightly more difficult element to the game. Today, the wind had picked up and at times the rain seemed to be blowing sideways.

We finished the first half in a 0-0 draw. Both sides had had some good chances. It seemed as if we had the advantage, as we'd managed to keep them from dictating play. But their defense had kept us out of their end more often than not.

"Jean," Coach said, "I'm moving you up to striker. Oz, you drop back to mid for now. We need to switch things up."

Oz looked upset by this, but he only said, "Okay, Coach."

"If they keep playing the way they are, we're going to need to start forcing play. They've had us in our end far too often. So let's stack up the midfield, four across, and we'll try a couple of dump and runs, all right?" Everyone nodded. We were too cold and wet to speak.

"Oz, it's going to be on your go, understand? Get firm control. Push forward, let one of their mids get behind you, then bomb it deep. Del and Jean, you two run hard. Give and go if you need to. But get it past their mids. Their defense is pulling up way too far. They're just asking for it." Coach gave Jared a clap on the back. "You stay solid, lad. No one's coming up the middle of that pitch. Got it?"

"Got it, Coach."

The play had sounded easy when Coach explained it. I was primed to shoot up the field at any moment. But every time the ball came close to Oz, he was surrounded by two or three opponents and was forced to pass it back to the defense. It was like the ball was doing circles for a while. Moving over to Oz, then back to the defense. Up the other side and back around.

Finally, Oz managed to navigate past one of the streaking strikers and got some air under the ball. Then one of the taller midfielders jumped and headed the ball back to our end. Jared caught it in midfield. He sent it back to Riley, who, in a moment of indecision, let it get knocked out of bounds.

As we all walked back for the throw-in, Coach caught my eye and made a quick gesture toward center field. I walked with everyone else, then drifted back to center as the ball was thrown in. Riley caught the ball in a roundhouse boot, which sent it flying upfield. It was moving slowly through the air, a gentle arc cutting through the rain.

I started running after it, blasting past the defense.

But they were fast, and as I got control of the ball, there was already someone kicking at my heels. The crowd was on its feet, yelling and clapping. I could see Jean coming up fast beside me. The keeper was moving out to cut me off, waving at his defense and shouting. Every time my right foot came back, I could feel the other player's toe on my heel. He caught me on the calf a couple of times.

"Jean!" I yelled, passing the ball over to him. He caught it on the inside of his left foot and moved toward the goal. It was like watching a professional player. The ball seemed to be attached to his foot by a string.

I quickly darted sideways, then stopped dead in the middle of the field. The defender blew past me, rushing at Jean. Another of their defenders had gone down in the mud. Jean turned his back to the defensive player, quickly moved downfield, then rifled a shot toward the goal.

I had begun running before the ball left his foot. The keeper came out to challenge, but he seemed to have misjudged where the ball was going. I launched myself into the air and headed the ball hard away from him.

Right into the top corner of the net.

The keeper had gone up at the same time, and I crashed into him after heading the ball. I heard the air being punched out of his chest upon impact. We landed in a heap as the other players closed in around us.

I was apologizing as I tried to get up when the keeper caught me in the side of the head with a quick, sharp punch.

"Goddamn dirty players," he said. I was holding the side of my face where he'd hit me. I tried to stand up to get away from the situation and he kicked me in the gut. I crumpled to the ground and started sucking mud.

"Hey!" someone yelled. And then I felt people moving around above me. People tripping on my crumpled form, stomping on me as they went at one another.

"Get off him!" someone yelled. I was trying to breathe. The kick to the gut had knocked the air out of me. Plus, there's not as much oxygen in mud as you might imagine. The whistle was screaming above me. Everyone was cursing. I could hear the slap of flesh on flesh. Then someone's hands were beneath my arms, pulling me up and dragging me away.

"That was a foul!" the keeper yelled. "This whole team's dirty. Everyone knows it."

"You okay, man?" Riley said. I managed to nod my head. He gave me a slap on the back. "Man, that was beautiful. Just perfect."

chapter fifteen

Mine was the only goal scored that game. The rest of the match fell to cheap shots and players yelling at one another. It was a contentious and dirty game, and I spent the remainder of the time on the bench with Romano.

We were lucky it didn't turn into an all-out brawl.

I honestly hate these kinds of games. When a bunch of people are angry with one another, skill takes a back seat.

In the end, it could have been anyone out there. All the players were doing was hoofing the ball back and forth, running at one another, slide tackling when the ball was already long gone and generally trying to cause injury.

"That was awful," Riley said when the game was over.

"We won," Jared said. "That's what matters. Above all else, brother." Riley gave him a fist bump. Jared bent down and helped Romano to his feet. Then he handed Oz Romano's crutches. "Carry these, man. I'll help Rom off the field." The other team's players were lingering between the stands. Their coach was out near the street, waiting for them to follow him.

"Go home," Jared said. "It's done here."

Some of the players started off toward the street. "You guys play dirty," the keeper yelled. "If you win, it's a dirty win. Does it mean that much to you?"

"Yeah," Riley yelled. "It does."

The keeper shook his head and walked away.

I waited for a few moments. There was something I didn't like about the whole situation. But my overall feeling was that I was soaking wet and filthy and just wanted to get changed.

When I got to the street, Elsa was there in her minivan. She waved me over.

"Come on, get in," she said.

I looked down at myself. I was a filthy mess. "Maybe a shower and stuff first?"

"We don't have time," she said. "We have to do something before it gets dark."

"I need to change though."

She opened the side door of the van and looked inside. "Here, I have a towel and a pair of shorts, and there's a shirt in here somewhere. We need to go."

"Where? What's going on?"

Riley was behind me. "Hey, Elsa," he said.

"Hey," she replied coldly.

"You coming, Del?" Riley said.

I looked at Elsa. She was staring at Riley. "No, um, Elsa and I have something to do," I said.

"Oh," Riley said. "Okay. Maybe catch you at the restaurant later?"

"Yeah, sure," I said. Elsa held the side door farther open and I hopped in. She got in the driver's seat and pulled away before I'd sat down. "I'm not changed yet or anything."

Elsa glanced in the rearview mirror. "We need to get out of here," she said.

"What's going on?" I put the towel around my waist and pulled off my soaking shorts. I dried myself off as best I could before pulling on Elsa's shorts. They were tight, but they fit.

"First off, you're wearing girls' shorts."

"Hey," I said.

"Just wanted to point it out."

"Like I have a choice." I pulled my shirt off and put hers on. It was pretty gender-neutral. Just a black shirt with white stripes on the sleeves. "What's going on?"

"How well do you know your friend Riley?"

"Pretty well," I said as I squeezed between the front seats. "Why?"

"What does his dad do?"

"He's a carpenter. Why?"

She was nodding to herself, watching me in the rearview. "My brother found this bar in the bushes near Romano's restaurant. It's used for prying nails out of things and pulling up plywood."

"A pry bar?"

"Yeah, sure, I guess."

"Okay. And your brother found it near the restaurant? What was he doing there?"

"After Doug was suspected, he went there to see if he could find anything."

"You mean like clues?"

"Exactly."

"And he just happened to find this pry bar?"

"Yeah. You sound like you don't believe me."

I didn't know what to believe. "Why didn't he just give it to the police?"

"Because he wanted Riley to admit to what he'd done first. He figured that would be a better way to do it. He's never touched it with bare hands. He was always wearing gloves."

I remembered how Evan had been wearing gloves the night we saw him at the mall. "Wait a minute. Did your brother know we were going to show up at the mall that night?"

"Yeah, apparently."

"How?"

"He told Kira where he was going to be. He knew she'd tell Riley. Kira's a drama queen. She likes to be, I don't know, the impetus for conflict."

"So of course she would tell Riley."

"Of course." We'd been set up. That much was evident. They'd wanted to talk to us as much as we'd wanted to talk to them.

"Wait a minute. So you think Riley took Romano out?"

Elsa glanced over at me. We'd hit the highway by this time and were heading west. "I notice you have a new player," she said.

"Yeah, Jean."

She nodded. "How did he get on your team?"

"We didn't have any subs, so the league allowed us to bring in a new player," I said.

"Sure, sure. But why him? How did anyone even know he could play?"

"I don't know," I said.

"Really?"

"No, I never asked anyone. Why? What do you know?" I said.

"A couple of weeks ago, my friend Dan was playing with Jean downtown when a couple of guys from your school showed up. They watched him play, Del. Dan heard them asking him if he'd be willing to play for their team."

"That doesn't mean anything," I said. "Who says it was Riley?"

"It could have been," she said. "It would add up."

"So what are we doing? Where are we going?"

"To get the pry bar and take it to the police."

"Where is it?"

"At the mall," she said. "Evan dropped it the other night when he got chased."

I did not want to go back into that mall. Once had been enough. "I'm not going back in there," I said. "That was brutal. There are all kinds of people in there. It's probably not even legal."

Elsa laughed. "Toughen up, soldier. We'll be in and out in fifteen minutes. Well before it gets dark. Don't worry your pretty little head."

chapter sixteen

The mall was only slightly less creepy in daylight. There was enough light coming through the skylights to do without flashlights, but it would soon be getting dark.

"Where did you guys run into my brother and his friends?" Elsa said.

"Just up here," I said. We were whispering to one another. The rain was pounding loudly on the roof and skylights.

"Evan said he dropped it when he ran. It caught on something and he just let it go."

We walked toward where we'd run into Evan and his friends. There was broken glass on the floor. It crunched beneath our feet, sounding like ice breaking on a frozen sidewalk.

Elsa grabbed my hand. "You were right—this is creepy," she said.

"I know," I whispered back. "People *live* in here."

"What? Where?"

I shouldn't have said anything. "Nowhere. Let's just get the pry bar." I directed her back to the spot where we'd had our confrontation. "What's this going to prove anyway?"

"The police will do fingerprinting on it."

"Okay."

"Evan said there was blood on it as well. They can match it with Romano's."

"Why are you so hell-bent on figuring out who did this?"

Elsa had been crouched down looking at the floor, but she glanced up at me then. "Why aren't you?"

"Romano's going to be okay," I said.

"But everyone thinks Doug had something to do with an assault. And he just wouldn't. It's not fair that he's unjustly accused."

"If he's such a nice guy, what was he doing with his best friend's girlfriend?" I said.

"That's beside the point," Elsa said. She wasn't looking at me anymore.

"Isn't it kind of exactly the point?" I said.

"How?"

"Well, if he lied about where he was and lied to his best friend about who he was with, what's keeping him from lying now?"

"Remember the pictures?"

"Like I said before, those could have been doctored."

Elsa came over to me. "Let's forget about all of this for now and just find this thing, okay? I want to get out of here." She leaned into me and gave me a quick kiss on the cheek. "Where could it be?"

I remembered how we'd all taken off in roughly the same direction, away from the three guys who had arrived.

"We all went this way," I said. We walked deeper into the mall. "Someone might already have taken it. A pry bar can be useful."

"We need to find it," Elsa said. "It has to be here somewhere." She was making a lot of noise, kicking things around and stomping on glass. We'd only been inside for ten minutes or so, but it was already getting dark. Soon we'd need flashlights. We hadn't even bothered to bring them inside.

"Didn't he tell you where he dropped it?" I said.

"He didn't tell me anything. No one knows I'm here."

"What?"

"Just find the stupid bar, Del."

"Let's just go," I said. I wanted to prove that Riley had nothing to do with any of this, but the mall was freaking me out. Plus, I wasn't even sure that finding the bar would make a difference.

"No," Elsa said. "It has to be here somewhere."

"We can tell the police," I said. "Let them know it's in here."

"The police aren't ever going to know that it was in here. We are going to bring it to them and tell them we found it in the bushes."

"What?" I said. "Why would we do that?"

"If they know it's been here, they'll just say it wasn't the weapon used in the attack. Don't you see?"

"No, Elsa, I don't see. What is really going on here?"

"I don't trust Riley. I don't trust him with Kira. I think he did this, and if he did, that's just creepy. He has to be held accountable. And Kira has to see what kind of a person he is."

"He's not a bad guy," I said.

"Well," she said, "I guess we'll find out."

"This is starting to feel like a witch hunt," I said. "I think we should just go."

She quickly dropped my hands. "Fine, go. Wait by the van. I'll be out as soon as I find the bar."

"I'm not leaving you in here alone," I said.

"Then help me find this stupid thing. It has to be here somewhere."

I was totally confused. But I didn't have much time to linger in indecision, because as we separated and began looking around, we heard the sound of breaking glass.

chapter seventeen

I took Elsa's hand and led her into the comic-book store I'd gone through last time. We crouched behind an overturned shelving unit.

"Who is that?"

"Probably the same guys who were here before," I said.

A face appeared at the accordion door. I didn't recognize the guy. He was wearing a torn T-shirt and looked like he'd just dragged himself out of a ditch somewhere.

It was dark enough inside, I hoped, that without a flashlight he wouldn't see us.

"I thought I saw something move in here," the guy said. He pulled on the doors, trying to separate them. He pushed a leg and part of his torso through before one of the other guys ran by and smacked him on the head.

"Get out of there, dillweed. There's no one here."

"Hey," the guy in the door said. "What's this?" He bent down and picked up a pry bar. "Hey guys!" he yelled before running toward his friends. "Guys, look what I found. We can smash stuff with this."

"Shit," Elsa whispered. "We have to get that." She stood up.

I pulled her back down. "Are you crazy? What, do you think they'll just give it to you?"

"We have to get it, Del. Let's at least follow them and see if they throw it down somewhere." She was through the accordion doors before I could stop her.

So I followed.

The guys had turned the next corner. It was dark in the mall now, and just as creepy as it had been the time before. I caught up with Elsa and reached for her arm.

"These are the same guys that were here last time," I said.

"So?"

"The guys who beat your brother up. The guys who think this is their clubhouse."

"We need that bar." We'd slipped in behind an overturned bench. I could see down the next corridor. It looked like there were five guys. They were smashing whatever they could and spray painting big, looping letters on every flat surface.

"Elsa," I said. "They are not going to drop that thing."

"Wait," she said. "They won't take it out with them." I heard a sound behind us and froze. There was a guy urinating on the wall. I had no idea why we hadn't seen him.

"Hey," he yelled. "What are you two doing in here?"

"Run," I said, grabbing Elsa's hand.

"Hey, guys, guys, over here. A couple of girls." The guy was fighting with his zipper.

I jumped over a planter and skidded on some broken glass. Elsa yanked me forward.

"Guys! Guys!"

"Head back to the comic-book store," I said.

"Why not the way we came in?" Elsa said.

"Trust me," I said. We got to the front of the comic-book store and slid between the accordion doors. As we were crashing through the store, two of the guys arrived at the doors.

"Ladies, where are you going? We're nice guys. Come on, stick around." One of the guys put the flashlight to his face, I guess trying to freak us out. I pulled Elsa through the store and hammered the back door with my forearm. It didn't pop open. I looked back. The first of the guys was pushing his way through the accordion doors. I hit the door again. The accordion doors were shivering as he and the others squirmed through.

"Hurry, Del. Hurry," Elsa said. I took a step back and kicked the security bar as hard as I could. The door popped open. Something crashed to the ground on the other side. We squeezed through the slim space and were out on the loading dock. Someone had piled a bunch of boxes and what looked like roofing tiles against the door.

"Which way?" Elsa said.

"To the van. Come on." We ran through the trees toward the road. The door slammed open behind us.

"Ladies!" one of the guys yelled. "Come back. We need you!" They were laughing like this was the funniest thing ever said. A moment later I heard their feet hit the ground, and they were chasing us.

We'd parked in much the same spot as Jared had before—a quiet, calm residential street. We got to the van, and Elsa fumbled with her keys. She dropped them and went down on her knees to get them. Six guys came crashing through the trees.

"Hurry," I said.

"I'm trying, Del," Elsa replied. The horn beeped and the locks disengaged. We got in and slammed the doors shut. Elsa put the key in the ignition.

"Lock the doors!" I said. She fumbled around the armrest. There was a thump on the back of the van. I looked over my shoulder and saw that one of the guys was pretending to be plastered to the rear window. He was laughing, his eyes wild.

Elsa managed to lock the doors just as another of the guys got to the side door and started pulling on the handle.

"Hey, come on. We need a ride."

"Go," I said.

"I'm trying, Del." She was crying as she turned the key in the ignition. The guys were banging on the van like wild apes.

"Let us in! Let us in!" The van started up and Elsa dropped it into drive, stomping on the gas. We tore away just as one of the guys took a swing at the rear taillight with the pry bar. I looked back as we swerved up the street. One of the guys was hopping around on one foot, clasping the other in his free hand.

"I think you ran over that guy's foot," I said.

"Dammit," Elsa replied.

"It's all right," I said. "He kind of had it coming."

"Not that," she said. "We didn't get the bar." She shot through a stop sign and a minute later we were on the highway, heading home.

chapter eighteen

We stopped beside this park around the corner from Romano's restaurant. Elsa turned off the van. When she took her hands off the steering wheel, I could see she was still shaking.

"Who were those guys?" she said.

"People just go in there to wreck the place," I said. "They could have been anyone. Same as last time. Those guys who beat up your brother were probably there to smash things and do whatever else they wanted to."

"Why?" she asked.

"I don't know—they're knobs."

She shook her head, unable to understand this. "Are you going to the restaurant?"

I looked out the window. "I don't really feel like it."

"So where are you going, then?"

I wanted to be suave and cool and say something like, *Wherever you're going, baby.* But instead I just said, "I don't know."

Elsa was silent as she stared out at the empty street.

"Doug isn't allowed to play. You know that, right?"

"No," I said. "I didn't."

"It's not fair."

Without thinking, I said, "I still don't get why you care so much."

"I care because Doug is my friend. Plus, he's this hugely talented soccer player. There are going to be scouts from a bunch of colleges at the final, and he won't be playing.

When they ask why he's not playing, they'll be told about the attack and how he may or may not be connected. What chance will he have of getting a scholarship then?"

"Likely not a great one."

"You have another year of high school, Del. The scouts will be back for you. They won't for Doug. And that's not fair. He didn't do anything."

I didn't know what to believe. If I were Doug, I wouldn't have risked everything to take out a mediocre player like Romano just because of some stupid disagreement on the field. But I wasn't Doug. That's the problem with trying to figure people out. You never know what's going through their heads.

"Well, we can take what we have to my coach and see—"

"Hey, is that Riley?" Elsa said. And, sure enough, it was. He rounded the corner and sat down on a bench. "What's he doing?"

"I don't know," I replied. I went to open the door. "I'll go see."

"No, wait." She put her hand on my leg. "He's looking at that house across the street. Do you know who lives there?"

I squinted at the house. "Yeah," I said. "That's Jared's place."

"He's on your team?"

"Yeah. He plays center."

"Let's wait a second and see what he does."

A few minutes later, a car pulled out of Jared's driveway. As the car passed us, I saw Jared's mother and father inside. Riley got up, crossed the street and walked up the driveway.

"Come on," Elsa said, getting out.

I got out my side and met her on the sidewalk. It was dark but no longer raining. The streetlights were glowing warmly on the wet ground.

Elsa moved up the street, staying close to the row of trees. When we got to the end of Jared's driveway, we stopped and listened. At first there was nothing. Then there was a quick popping and the tinkle of breaking glass.

"What was that?" Elsa said.

I looked around the hedge and saw Riley going into Jared's garage. A light flashed on inside, and I could see that a pane of glass in the door had been broken.

I looked up and down the street, then walked up to the garage and stepped inside.

"What are you doing, Riley?" I said.

Riley was bent down beneath a table, digging through a box of tools. He spun around and looked at me wide-eyed.

"What are you doing here, Del?" He stood up and darted to the door. "Is anyone with you?"

"Elsa," I said.

"Were you two following me?"

"We just happened to be—"

"You just happened to be watching Jared's house. Sure," Riley said. He kicked the door closed.

"What's going on, Riley?"

He shook his head a couple of times, then went back to digging through the box. "I can't say anything, Del. Just get out of here before someone catches us."

I leaned against a table as Elsa came into the garage.

"Shut the door," Riley said. Elsa closed the door behind her.

I decided to get it out in the open immediately. "Did you do it?" I said.

"Did I do what?"

"Did you take Romano out?"

He shook his head. "Why would you even think that?"

"Because you knew about Jean, right? You met him before, and you knew how good he was. And you were angry at Romano for blowing that game for us. You...you really want to win."

He turned around and stood up. "We all want to win, Del. Winning is all that matters."

Then I remembered something else.

"You used to take martial arts," I said.

"Yeah, so?"

"So you probably learned how to choke someone out."

Riley laughed. "I told you, I wasn't very good at that." He went to a bench and started moving things around. I noticed he was wearing gloves.

"Are you looking for a pry bar?" I said.

He stopped knocking things around and turned to me. "What do you know about it?"

"We know it's gone," Elsa said.

"Gone where?"

"It doesn't matter. It's gone. Is that what you're looking for in here? Did Jared have it?"

The door shot open. Jared was standing in the doorway.

"Did I have what?" he said.

chapter nineteen

"What the hell, guys? Who broke my window? What are you doing in here?" Jared said.

"I'm looking for the pry bar, Jared," Riley said. He stood up, and I could tell he was nervous. He always starts rubbing his wrist when he's nervous.

"What pry bar?" Jared said.

"The one you stole from my father," Riley said. "The one you used to crush Romano's ankle."

"I have no idea what you're talking about."

Riley looked at me. "Remember I told you about those martial-arts lessons I used to take? Well, Jared was in that class too. And he kept taking them once I'd quit."

"So?" Jared said.

"So you know how to knock someone unconscious. And you know exactly where to hit someone to bruise the bone."

"Are you accusing me of something?" Jared said. He hadn't moved from the doorway, but he was standing straight and tall.

"Where's the pry bar?" Riley said again. "The day after Romano was attacked, my dad needed it and it was gone."

"My brother found a pry bar in the bushes the morning after the attack," Elsa said. "Kind of stupid to leave the weapon at the scene, isn't it?"

"Who is she?" Jared asked.

I didn't feel like introducing Elsa at that moment. "Is this all true, Jared?" I said.

"You guys think I took Romano out? Man, that's cold. Why would I do that?"

"Because you need to win, Jared," I said. "You need to win more than anything. And Romano was becoming a liability. He was making stupid plays and injuring people. Plus, with Jean in the wings, you figured it was fine to take a chance."

"Seriously, guys, I wouldn't do that. Rom's my friend. He's part of the team."

"I know you took the pry bar," Riley said. "I remember you looking at it. And right after you left, I thought I saw someone in our garage. That was you, wasn't it?"

"If I did take it, why would I leave it in the bushes as you claim?" Jared asked, turning to Elsa. "Why not do a better job of hiding it?"

"Because it didn't matter to you if the pry bar was found or not," Riley said. "If it was, your fingerprints wouldn't be on it, but my dad's would be. He puts a sticker on all his tools with his name and address. And you knew that too. You asked about it when we were in the garage. You wore gloves all the time, didn't you?"

"He did," I said, thinking back to the restaurant. "When I was leaving that night, he had the team's keeper gloves on."

"You were wearing them the day you were at my place too," Riley said. "I remember that when you left, you said they were new and you were working them in for Alvaro."

"What time did you leave the restaurant?" I said.

"I'm not answering any of these questions," Jared said. "It's stupid to think that I would have done that. Romano's my friend and teammate." He backed out of the doorway and pointed at the broken glass. "You're going to have to pay for this."

"Doug isn't going to be able to play in the final tomorrow," Elsa said.

"Good," Jared replied.

"He didn't do anything."

"We don't know that," Jared replied.

"You know he didn't," she said.

"I don't know anything about it. I don't like being accused of this either. I thought we were friends, man."

Elsa walked past him and stood in the driveway.

"You know this isn't the right way to do it, Jare," I said. "We can win without cheating." He didn't reply. I thought Riley was going to hit him on his way past. But Riley's half his size and more of a human being than Jared will ever be.

When we got to the sidewalk, Riley said, "He's right. We can't prove anything."

"I heard the bell ring twice right before Romano was attacked. But you said you couldn't get into the restaurant. So where was Jared? Did you see him?"

"I didn't see anyone inside the restaurant. But I heard the bell ring twice too."

"But you didn't see anyone come out?" Elsa said.

"No."

"Do you think he was going to try and pin it on you?" I said as we neared Elsa's minivan.

"I had a feeling," he said. "I mean, if it ever looked as if he was going to be busted for it or even questioned, yeah,

153

he would have pointed a finger at me right away."

"So what were you going to do?" Elsa asked.

Riley shrugged. But there was too much in that shrug. Too much indecision.

"Were you going to tell Coach?"

"I really didn't know what I was going to do," he said. "I just needed to get the pry bar back. I guess I hadn't thought beyond that."

Elsa opened the van. "You have to tell your coach what you know," she said. She got in and started the engine. "Or I will." She slammed the door shut and drove off.

"What a mess," I said as we watched her drive away.

"Yeah," Riley said. "It sure is."

chapter twenty

The scouts were in the stands again. They were typing away on tablets or talking into cell phones when we took the field.

At first they made me nervous. But then I realized that Elsa was right. I had another year to impress people. Another year of playing and getting better.

Eventually, I forgot they were there and focused on the game.

The Rebels were playing an incredibly disciplined game. They were taking possession time away from us and winning all the battles. They had three corner kicks in the first half alone. They never managed to score, but it didn't seem to matter. They were the better team, and that's often enough.

We left the field at the half feeling like the underdogs. The weather was perfect for once. Bright and sunny, but not sweltering. Because the Rebels had finished first, we were playing on their field. The stands were much newer than the ones at our school, and they were filled with spectators. The atmosphere was one of excitement and anticipation.

"What's going on out there?" Coach said. "We're losing all the battles that matter. We're falling apart. Help me out here—where did the team go?"

"They're playing hard, Coach," Oz said.

"And so are we." He looked at the pitch. "Get into the cycling game. Move the ball around more. And don't give it up." He was at a loss for what to do. That much was evident. You can't play a cycling game when you don't have possession. We were spending the majority of our time running the ball down and blocking shots. And there was no reason to believe the Rebels wouldn't be coming on just as strong in the second half.

"What about the flip play?" Jared said. Our regular keeper had broken his toe chasing his dog around, and Jared was our backup, so not only were we down to no subs, but we also had a less than fantastic keeper making everyone nervous and overly cautious.

I didn't look at Jared. I hadn't been able to talk to him since we'd discovered what had happened to Romano. I had wanted to tell Coach about it, but I couldn't. We didn't have any proof.

"Good idea, lad. These guys didn't see that one before." He clapped Jean on the back. "Jean, you go to the center and just wait it out. Del, hang back a touch."

"I can send it that far," Jared said. "I've done it before."

"Whoever gets the ball, hold it, wait them out, then send it."

For the first five minutes, I swear we didn't touch the ball. We were playing to win, but the Rebels had something to prove. Doug was on the sidelines. He never sat down once, as far as I could tell. He was cheering his team on. Willing them forward.

Romano was on our bench, looking sullen and beat. I wondered if he had begun to suspect who it was that had attacked him. Maybe Jared had been too nice to him. Said something he shouldn't have. Known more than he was supposed to.

We were ten minutes in when the Rebels scored. It was a beautiful sweeping move by one of their strikers after a corner kick. The third corner kick in a row.

Coach became more animated than ever. Clapping and stomping around. Yelling at us. He normally remained calm on the sidelines. Stoic, even. But he was losing it out there that day.

"Drop play!" Jared yelled as we moved upfield. "Del, drop!" I ignored him. "This is yours, man!"

The ball came into play, and we managed to get deep into their end when one of their defenders won a one-on-one battle with Jean and booted the ball back into our end.

Jared came way out of his goal and brought the ball down. Then he just stood there with it at his feet. He was outside the box and couldn't pick it up. The first striker was on him immediately. He deked the guy out and ran the ball to the right side. The Rebels began pushing toward him. There's nothing more enticing than an open net, and our net was as open as it could be. All anyone had to do was steal the ball from Jared and boot it in.

He deked another player, then ran the ball to center and, in one swift motion, sent it flying high and deep.

I started to run.

My mind emptied of all thoughts. Everything that had happened over the previous weeks. The attack, Elsa, the mall, Jared. All of it disappeared as I focused on the ball hovering up there, then beginning its descent. I was past all but one of the defenders as the ball came down. I jumped just as the defender was about to launch himself at it and tapped it to the ground with a quick header.

Jean was right there, crossing the field and moving on toward the goal. I went to the opposite side, waiting for the cross if it was to come.

But it didn't. Jean slipped the ball between the keeper's legs and tied the game.

Jared came up the field and threw his arms around Jean and me.

"Well done," he said. "Nice." He let go and yelled, "Let's go, let's get another."

As he ran back toward our goal, I was struck with a memory. I didn't know why, but for a moment I was transported back to the restaurant on the night Romano was attacked. It was an uneventful memory. I was just sitting in the booth and Jared was beside me.

Then I found the missing piece.

Jared's cologne.

He wore this very strong and distinct cologne. He prided himself on it.

"Coach!" I yelled. "Time-out!" Coach held his hands up, questioning. "We need a time-out!" I yelled again. He shrugged and called to the ref. I ran over to where Romano was sitting on the bench.

"Rom," I said. "Do you remember smelling anything when you were attacked?"

"Smelling what?" Romano said.

"Cologne," I said.

"What?"

"What's this all about, Del?" Coach said.

"Jared was the one who attacked Romano," I said.

"What are you talking about?" Coach said.

"No one saw him do it. But it was him. I'm sure of it. Think back, Romano. Did you smell Jared's cologne?"

Romano looked up. The rest of the team had circled around us.

The ref started yelling at us that our time was up.

"I don't know what this is all about, but we have to get back out on the field. Let's just play on," Coach said.

"It's not right, Coach," I said. "Jared did it, and Doug is sitting out. He didn't do anything, and he's stuck on the bench."

"Shut up, Del," Jared said. He came up and shoved me. Romano looked up at him. The smell of Jared's cologne was everywhere. "You don't know what you're talking about."

"I do," I said, wondering if I'd made a huge mistake confronting him right here on the field.

"We can deal with this after the game," Coach said.

"We can't," I said. I got down on one knee in front of Romano. "Rom, you have to tell him. If we're going to win this, we have to win it fairly."

"How is that even possible now?" Rom said.

"It isn't. But if Doug doesn't get to play and Jared does, that's totally unfair."

Romano looked at Jared. He inhaled deeply. "You're right, that was the smell," he said, his cheeks starting to redden. "I'd been trying to place it. Trying to remember where I'd smelled it before. But that was the smell."

He stood up and shoved Jared. "What the hell, Jared?"

"Shut up, Rom. Why would I do that to you?" Jared yelled.

Rom fell back to the bench and grabbed at his ankle. "Because you want to win."

Everyone was looking at Jared.

"Where were you when Rom was attacked?" Coach asked.

"Home," Jared said.

"You couldn't have been," Riley said. "I heard you leave no more than a minute before Rom came outside. Right, Romano?"

"Maybe two minutes, but, yeah, he'd just left."

"So I was on my way home. What's the difference?"

"You weren't, Jared," I said. "You waited for Romano to leave, then you choked him out and clobbered his ankle with the pry bar you stole from Riley."

"Where is all this coming from?" Coach said.

"None of it's true!" Jared said. "They don't have any proof!"

"It is," I said. I stood up and looked at Coach. "We should have come to you before. But it's all true."

"Rom?" Coach said. He put his hand on Romano's shoulder. "Do you know for certain it was Jared?"

"I didn't see him, but that was definitely his cologne I smelled." Rom turned away from Coach and shook his head at Jared. "Why'd you do it, man? I wasn't playing hard enough for you?"

"Because winning was top priority and Jared had already spotted a better player," I said.

"What's this?" Coach asked.

"Jared knew how good Jean was. He'd seen him play downtown."

"And then you brought him straight to me," Coach said to Jared. "Lad, what were you thinking?"

The ref was standing in front of us now.

"I have to get this game going again," he said. "What's the holdup?"

Coach put his hand on the shoulder of Greg, one of our defensive players, and said, "You're in net."

"What? No way!" Jared said. "These are all lies. I didn't do anything!"

"Go to the showers," Coach said. "You're done."

"You have no proof," Jared yelled.

I couldn't look at him.

"Fine," Jared said. "Lose." Then he stormed off.

"Is there something I should know about here?" the ref asked.

"The lad there on the bench?" Coach said, pointing at Doug. "He had nothing to do with the attack on our player. He should be allowed to play."

"I don't think I can make that call," the ref said. "That came down from the league. And the police."

"Anything comes of it, you hang it on me. He had nothing to do with the attack. We're sure of it."

The ref went to the other bench and filled the coach in on the events. Eventually, he blew his whistle and we took to the field again, one man short.

chapter twenty-one

We learned a lot that day. First of all, Greg is about the worst keeper you can imagine. We also learned that you can lose and walk off a field with your head high.

And we really did lose, 4-1.

It was actually pretty embarrassing.

Jared had cleared out of the change room by the time the rest of us arrived. I'd felt totally alone as we walked off the field, but when the door closed behind us, Oz came over and put a hand on my back.

"You did the right thing, Del," he said. "And you played a hell of a game too."

"Thanks."

Riley sat down beside me on the bench. "I bet Jared is pretty angry now."

I shrugged. "Let him be. You okay about not winning?"

"I guess. Winning would have been better though."

"But not that way."

While we were outside waiting for the team bus to arrive, Kira pulled up and rolled the window down.

"Need a ride?" she said.

I looked at Riley. "I think she means you."

"Sure," he said. "Where's Elsa?"

Kira opened the passenger's-side door. "I don't know."

Riley got in and closed his door.

"Wait a second," I said. "Could you drop me off somewhere?"

"Sure," Kira said. I slid into the back seat and waited for Kira and Riley to disengage their lips from one another.

I directed her to Beacon Hill Road and had her drop me at the path leading to the lifts.

"What are you going to do up here?" Riley asked.

"Think," I said. He looked at me strangely. I bent down beside the window. "Sorry I ever thought it could have been you." Riley put his fist out the window. I gave it a quick bump.

"No worries," he said.

I stepped back from the door and Kira gunned it down the hill.

I passed Elsa's van in the parking lot and carried on to the lifts. Elsa was on the top chair, staring straight ahead at the city below. I could tell she'd noticed me coming.

"Hey," I said when I got to her. "You want company?"

"Sure," she said. "How did you know I would be here?"

"I was actually just really hoping," I said as I hopped up. "Otherwise, it would be a long walk home." She shifted slightly away from me, and what I had been suspecting cemented in my gut. "You have some thinking to do?"

"Yeah," she said. She had only briefly looked at me and given me a very quick, very fake smile.

"Does he know?" I said.

"Who?"

"Doug."

She looked at me then. "Know what?"

"That you like him?"

It seemed as if she was going to deny it but then changed her mind.

"No," she said.

"So what was this all about?" I asked. "You and me."

"I like you, Del," she said. "That's what it was about. Just, I guess, not in the same way." I thought about it for a moment, and it made sense. Elsa had been hell-bent on proving Doug's innocence since the beginning. But I doubted she was ever trying to use me.

"Okay," I said. "I don't think he's really right for you anyway."

"You don't even know him," she said.

She would keep on thinking this, I figured. That she knew him better than anyone else. That she knew what he was *really* like. The same way Rom had convinced himself it couldn't have been Jared who took him out. The same way I had never wanted to believe it could possibly have been Riley.

"No, I guess not."

She took a deep breath, then grabbed my hand and held it. It was getting dark enough that the city was beginning to blink with streetlights. We watched rows of them flash on in the distance. We stayed there a long time, not saying anything. Just watching the city switch from day to night.

"Hey," she finally said. "Don't you owe me an ice cream?"

"Why?"

"From that night? The deal we had?"

"No way," I said. "We were tied, if I remember correctly. Or maybe I was in the lead." She squeezed my hand. "Rematch?"

"Deal."

Jeff Ross is the author of four previous YA novels, all with Orca Book Publishers. He teaches scriptwriting and English at Algonquin College in Ottawa, where he lives with his wife and two kids. His previous books have been listed on the CCBC's Best Books for Teens and YALSA's Quick Picks for Reluctant Young Readers. His soccer skills have been in question since he was six, but sometimes determination is more important than skill. Right?

Acknowledgments

Thanks go out to Amy Collins for her incredible editing of this book. And to Elsa and Kira for loaning their names (but not their personalities—don't worry, girls).